Golf Dogs

Buzz Rettig

ISBN: 1719040885
ISBN-13: 9781719040884

DEDICATION

To my wife and best friend Maggie, for her love, patience, and encouragement.

CONTENTS

ACKNOWLEDGMENTS

Thanks to Andrew Miller for his artwork and Joyce Ward for her clean-up, and to my family and friends for their encouragement, suggestions, and support.

THE END OF MAY

Travis Dempsey muttered angrily as he scanned the thick, matted grass around his feet. It was like a huge comb-over; three-foot grass bent by wind and rain, and trampled daily by other golfers whose shots had strayed from the fairway.

"Damn it!" He kicked at the thick tufts of green to the left of the fairway. He was pretty sure that his ball had landed around here...somewhere...but from two hundred and twenty yards away, with aging eyes, who could tell? It's the price you pay for playing this stupid game, he thought. And for getting old.

He trudged through the dense grass, head down, blue eyes focused on the ground. His ball cap, tilted back on his head, exposed thick blonde hair. In his early forties, he was still in good shape, his nearly six foot frame carrying little fat, though his waist was beginning to show the nascent signs of 'deskitis', an unavoidable inflammation brought on by success and inactivity.

"I think it's gone, Travis." Vincent Verdu, a short, bullish man searching the grass twenty feet further on, looked to his friend with round, sympathetic eyes. "You'll need to take a drop."

Dempsey hissed in frustration. He'd lost two balls already, and they'd only played nine holes. He was going to have to open another sleeve of balls at the turn.

"If it's any consolation," offered Rex Clawson, his southern accent honeyed with sarcasm, "it was a fine drive, right up until it took that nasty turn and vanished into the smegma."

Clawson was of medium height and medium build. His only vices were single women, single malt scotch, and a tendency to playfully bait his friends during golf.

"Tell me again what smegma is?" Dempsey tossed another ball towards the fairway.

"Christ, Travis," cried Verdu in mock protest, "that's a pretty generous drop."

"Leave the man alone." This from Mitch Pearsall, the fourth in their group. He was standing on the edge of the fairway to ensure that the following foursome wouldn't drive up on them. At six and a half feet tall, deep ebony skin, a clean-shaven head, and a fashion sense that favored garish Hawaiian shirts, he was the designated fairway beacon when play stopped to search for errant shots. "He's got enough on his mind without you busting his balls."

"I'm not bustin' his balls," clarified Verdu. "Just questioning where he drops 'em."

"Smegma," Clawson interrupted, moving towards his cart to select a club, "is any thick, unforgiving grass or weedy accumulation that grasps unsuspecting golf balls and hides them from their rightful owner."

"Sure," Verdu laughed, nodding. "Smegma."

"You know," Dempsey said, pulling a club from his bag and addressing the ball, "where I come from, smegma has an entirely different, and not-for-mixed-company meaning."

"I am well aware of the definition you refer to," Clawson sneered, his accent thickening. "But I am not responsible for how badly you Yankees have bastardized an otherwise genteel language. In the south, we would never be so crude or crass."

Pearsall smiled. "You have to protect the purity and honor of those southern belles, right?"

"Absolutely!" Clawson gave his tall friend a casual wink. "Though, as you have no doubt surmised, I am not a mother's first choice to protect either their belle's purity or honor."

Dempsey took a slow, measured swing at the ball. The club head struck the ball solidly, sending it on its one hundred and eighty yard trek towards the green. The ball sailed gracefully towards the hole, and looked to be a perfect recovery shot from the rough…until it began drifting left. And then the drift became a turn, a sharp turn. Dempsey's ball bounced once on the fringe of the fairway, then raced for cover like a mouse sensing the rapid decent of a hawk, vanishing into the calf-high grass on the other side of the fairway.

"Shit!"

"The grass grabbed your club," Verdu observed, moving off to take his shot. Like the others in the foursome, his ball was in the fairway.

"Bad luck," Clawson offered.

Pearsall looked over his shoulder. The foursome behind them were ready to tee off.

"Let's take our shots," he said. "We're slowing play."

* * * * *

Verdu signaled the waitress for another round.

"The thing about golf," he began, "is that some days you can do no wrong, and some days you should just have stayed home."

The four men were sitting in the clubhouse, their round finished and their scores entered into the club's handicap database. It had been one of Dempsey's worst days ever, one of Pearsall's best, and a pleasant walk, with the occasional golf swing thrown in for good measure, for Clawson and Verdu.

"You're not going to give us more of your golf philosophy, are you?" Clawson downed the remains of his Cragganmore.

"Might as well," Dempsey said. Not much of a drinker, he nursed his beer. "After a day like today, philosophy is all I have."

"It's just a game," Pearsall reminded his friends.

"See what I mean?" Dempsey pointed accusingly at his law partner.

"Easy for you to say," Verdu challenged, good-naturedly. "You were amazing out there today."

Pearsall graced his friends with an impish grin. "I *was* godlike, wasn't I?"

Even Dempsey couldn't hold back a laugh. "It was a good round," he acknowledged.

The waitress brought their drinks. They toasted Pearsall's game.

"And next week," Pearsall declared, "one of you gentlemen will carry the team. Today was my day to shine. For our next round, who knows where the gods will turn their loving gaze?"

"Exactly." Verdu beamed, his round face becoming all teeth and no eyes. It was the most disarming aspect of the otherwise fierce looking man. His thickset, muscular frame gave him a youthful, though menacing appearance, in no way dispelled by his close cropped silver hair or the steady, unflinching set of his cool gray eyes. He looked exactly like the dockworker he'd started life as, and had learned early on that carrying yourself like you were ready for trouble often helped you avoid it. It was an approach to life that he'd never outgrown, or seen a need to. He looked more like a fifty-year-old stevedore than the sixty-two year old President and CEO of V&V Enterprises, a successful international moving, storage, and trans-shipment conglomerate, and one of Dempsey and Pearsall's most important clients.

Beneath the alarming exterior, though, was a gentle, kind soul, a loyal friend, father, and dotting husband whose utter lack of pretense was both refreshing and beguiling. He could be every bit as tough as his five foot, four inch, heavily muscled frame hinted at, but was rarely seen without a smile on his face, and never heard to utter a harsh or unkind word, even during his darkest, most abysmal rounds on the course.

"So next week," Clawson opined, "ol' Mitch could break

seventy!"

Pearsall snorted. "In my dreams. It's a fluke I played so well today."

"You were on fire," Dempsey observed, reaching over and patting his friend on the shoulder. "You could have squibbed a shot directly away from the pin and still ended up with no worse than a bogey."

"I wasn't quite that good," Pearsall protested.

Clawson shrugged, producing the card from his pocket, nodding as he reviewed the numbers.

"You never did worse than a bogey all day," he noted. "Nine bogeys, seven pars, and two birdies. That's a solid seventy-nine."

"Unlike Mr. Dempsey's score."

Dempsey shook his head in embarrassed amazement. "Thanks for reminding me, Vince."

"Ah, come on, Travis," Clawson teased. "It's not like you suck all the time."

"Hell," Vince stated, hoping to encourage his friend, "five of those strokes were from lost balls..."

"...and another five from shots that went out-of-bounds..."

"...not to mention that your short game stayed home..."

"...and you were struggling off the tee," Pearsall concluded.

"But other than that," Clawson deadpanned, "you weren't doing so badly."

Travis couldn't help but smile. There was something about the game that brought out the well-meaning smart ass in everyone. He did it himself, when he wasn't the dog on the team.

"You're right," he admitted, sipping his beer, "but I'm going to have to play a hell of a lot better if we're going to beat Muck and his crew this year."

Each man nodded thoughtfully.

"They cheat, you know?" Vince voiced what nearly every member of the Van Courtland Glen Country Club had come to understand. "But unless we can prove it..."

"...and others have tried..."

"…unsuccessfully…"

"…we'll just have to play at the top of our forms."

"So," Clawson asked, "the madness begins next week?"

Of the four men at the table, Clawson was the youngest, and the most recent member of the club. Unlike Verdu, Rex Clawson had been born to wealth and privilege, but had been raised with a strong Protestant ethic, a clear understanding of his place in the world, and an appreciation for the reality that a man of means, though not required to work, must always account for himself and generously contribute to society. They were lessons that he lived daily, contributing both time and money to a dozen charitable causes in and around Fredericksburg.

Hailing originally from Charleston, South Carolina, he was an unremarkable man in appearance, only two inches taller than Verdu, but there was something about the mix of his wavy black hair, his playful brown eyes, and his distinctive Southern accent that women found irresistible. Being on the friendly side of forty, and wealthy, didn't hurt his chances with the ladies, either. And while he might easily be perceived as the poster boy for the idle rich, those who knew him best, like his golf buddies, knew Clawson to be a decent, modest man of means who gave generously of his time and resources.

Even so, he wasn't beyond using his wealth to personal benefit, especially when it came to the game of golf.

An avid golfer since the age of five, Clawson's name and lineage had made no impression on the Van Courtland Glen Country Club Membership Committee when he'd first moved to Fredericksburg. The waiting list for membership, he'd been told, was quite long. The committee, however, shortened the list considerably when faced with Clawson's cashier's check for five times the princely membership fee.

Almost from the beginning, Clawson, a reserved, easy-going man, had gravitated to Dempsey and Pearsall. Evenly matched on the course, the three were just as compatible in temperament and outlook.

"Yes," Verdu acknowledged, "the madness begins."

The madness referred to was the annual Van Courtland Glen Golf Tournament. Open to members only, the tournament began on Memorial Day, and ended on Labor Day weekend. On the Sunday before the holiday, the club held its formal awards dinner to celebrate another successful tournament and honor its players. The winners received trophies. They also got reserved parking spaces for the year. But what the winners of the annual tournament played for, what meant more than the trophies and the glory, were the bragging rights.

"And if we can beat Muck and his toadies…" Pearsall hissed, his head bowed over his drink.

"That would be the best!" Dempsey's statement was met with reverential nods.

Clawson looked around the table at his friends. The faces he saw betrayed defeat before the starting bell.

"You guys are pathetic."

"You've played Muck, Rex." Verdu's voice rose slightly. "The guy's good."

"He's an asshole," corrected Clawson, "and he cheats."

"That's never been proven," Pearsall cautioned. "And even if he does, that still leaves Baxter, Pfunke, and Howe."

"They all cheat," Clawson insisted. "I've seen Pfunke shave strokes. And I've seen Howe improve his lie."

Dempsey waved his hand dismissively. "We've all done that."

"I'm not talking about pushing a ball out of a divot, Travis. I've seen Howe tee up his ball in the middle of the fairway on par fives."

"Clever," Pearsall acknowledged. "Use your driver back-to-back, get on in two."

"All of which means nothing," Dempsey said. "They're the team to beat. We know they're going to cheat. We need to figure out some way to beat them."

The four men went silent, the noise of the bar a minor distraction to their thoughts.

"Well," suggested Vince, "*we* could cheat."

"That had occurred to me, as well." Pearsall nodded at

his short friend.

Where Verdu was short and muscular, Pearsall was tall and lean.

Mitch Pearsall had always been tall, and his parents had harbored hopes of their son becoming a superstar of the NBA. Even as he'd entered Georgetown Law School on an academic scholarship, his folks had been guardedly optimistic that the young man would come to his senses and sign up for the NBA draft. The problem was that Mitch Pearsall had no interest in basketball, either as a participant or spectator. He had always wanted to be a lawyer.

While at Georgetown, Pearsall had been drawn to litigation, his easy going, good-natured temperament the perfect balance to his imposing appearance and sharp mind. He'd also become fast friends with another quick witted, ambitious law student who was his only match in moot court. In fact, he and Travis Dempsey had first met at opposite ends of a moot case, a case that each had sworn to win. It had not been a pretty trial, though Pearsall had ultimately taken the day. It was that event, though, that had initially bonded the two young men in friendship, a friendship that had grown and deepened during their time at Georgetown, and lasted well beyond, when each had gone on to seek their individual fame and fortune.

Successful in their own rights, they had kept in touch over the years, Dempsey settling in Fredericksburg, and Pearsall in Chicago. At an ABA meeting one year, Pearsall had mentioned to his friend that the fast paced life of the Windy City no longer held much charm for him, his wife, Nancy, or the kids. Did Travis have any ideas?

The timing couldn't have been better.

Dempsey was in the process of leaving his firm to open his own practice. The thought of going into business alone had been daunting, but Dempsey was committed to making it on his own. The prospect of having Pearsall at his side made opening a business seem somehow less threatening, and since neither man could think of anyone else they would rather be in business with, the decision had been made quickly and with no regrets. It had been a wise decision on both men's parts, and the resulting partnership had made both of them financially secure, successful, and very happy.

"The thought of cheating had occurred to us all, Mitch," corrected Dempsey, "just as we all agree that it really isn't an option."

"Why not?" Clawson was the picture of innocence.

Pearsall answered solemnly. "We play golf because of the challenge it presents to each of us. If you accept the basic premise that golf is a game where you are competing against yourself, then to cheat at the game is to cheat oneself."

Vince finished his drink. "You just made that up, didn't you."

"Besides," Dempsey added, "we're no good at cheating. At least, I'm not. I'm not sure I'm clever enough to figure out a way to cheat and get away with it."

"And you call yourself a lawyer?" Pearsall sneered, shaking his head.

Clawson nodded. "I see the point," he acknowledged, "though you would think four intelligent guys, such as ourselves, could figure something out."

"I have a solution," Vince stated. "We play the best golf we can and hope someone catches Muck."

"I think you're right," Dempsey agreed, "though I don't hold out much hope that Muck is going to be caught."

"Let's not worry about Muck," Pearsall said. "We win, we lose, we at least have the satisfaction of knowing that we played straight up." He shrugged. "If Muck can take pride in such a shallow victory, well, that's his problem."

"He's been taking pride in his shallow victories for years," Clawson observed.

"Still," Vince hissed, "it would be nice if someone got the guy by the balls and gave 'em a good squeeze."

The other men nodded their agreement, each creating a picture of the event in their mind.

"Speaking of balls," Clawson began, "we won't have a chance at anything if ol' Travis, here, keeps losing his."

They all laughed, but it had been on Dempsey's mind all day. He'd never lost that many balls in one round before. With the tournament coming, he wasn't anxious for a repeat.

*   *   *   *   *

Dinner at the Dempsey house was filled with subdued enthusiasm. The Dempsey children, Lauren and Cliff, could barely contain their excitement about the ending of school and the coming summer. Both children had inherited their love of the outdoors and athletics from their parents, and during the summer months they were constantly out and on the go; Lauren was a swimmer, and Cliff could always manage to find a game of sandlot baseball that needed a shortstop or centerfielder.

Donna Dempsey, Travis' wife, was a petite, athletic blond whose love for gardening was surpassed only by her love for her husband and children. During the spring, summer, and fall, when she wasn't shuttling the kids to their various activities, playing golf at the club, tennis with friends, or attending the odd social function required of the wife of the co-owner of Dempsey, Pearsall & Associates, she was up to her elbows in dirt. She loved the texture and aromatic promise of freshly turned earth. Her touch was as green as a summer forest, regardless of what she planted, and rare was the summer night when the Dempsey family didn't dine on freshly picked vegetables from the garden, or enjoy a floral setting grown and arranged specifically as the centerpiece for their dinner table. There was nothing she couldn't grow, which was a source of personal pride for Donna, and respectful awe from her family.

The only one in the family who cared little for Donna's gardening prowess, the kids athletic ability, the end of school, or Travis' legal skills, was Arnie P., the Dempsey's four year old Jack Russell Terrier. As bright and spry as a puppy, Arnie P. lived for the Dempseys, and was truly at ease only when the family was all accounted for, like now.

From his bed in the corner of the kitchen, Arnie P. listened to the family chattering. He had little sense of what was being said, but there was no mistaking the sounds of happiness, humor, and love.

"So swim club starts next Saturday?" Travis addressed the question to his fourteen-year old daughter.

"Friday," she corrected, wisps of her blond hair falling into her eyes. "School ends Thursday."

"Yeeessssss," hissed Cliff, joyfully. He pumped his arm like Tiger Woods sinking a thirty-foot putt.

"A little excited, Champ?"

"A lot," the eleven year old clarified. "I should have about five teams organized by the end of the week. We should be able to play ball every day this summer."

Donna' eyes grew in amazement. "You've organized five baseball teams?"

The boy nodded, gleefully chewing his meal.

Travis shook his head. "My son, the Commissioner of Sandlot."

"Enlightened self-interest," Lauren explained. It was clear that the phrase was one she'd learned, probably in school, but had not yet had an appropriate context in which to use it. She couldn't help but be pleased with herself, just as her parents couldn't help smiling.

"Enlightened self-interest," queried Travis, using his best lawyerly tone.

Lauren and Cliff nodded in unison, though the quick look the brother shot his sister made it clear that he had no idea what she was talking about, but that he trusted her enough to let her drive on this occasion.

"Cliff doesn't want to waste time organizing baseball teams, but knows that no one else is doing it." Lauren took a sip of milk. "All he wants to do is play ball all summer."

Cliff nodded, working a mouthful of food into submission.

"The only way to ensure that," the sister continued, "is to organize the teams himself. Once that's done, he gets to play."

She reached over and patted her brother's head

playfully. "You're so clever," she cooed.

"Get off," he said, shaking his head. Cliff didn't mind his sister touching him, but he was an eleven-year old male and there were certain protocols to be observed. Especially in front of the parents.

"Well," Travis said, winking at his wife, "I'm impressed."

"Me, too," Donna echoed. "But don't forget, either of you, that school may be out, but you'll still have things to do around here."

"We remember," Lauren said.

"How can we forget," mumbled Cliff.

"Cliff!" Travis tried to be stern.

"We get the same lecture every year," Cliff protested, "but we always do whatever it is you want us to do."

"You would agree that we have to do a bit more than our share of reminding," Donna countered.

Cliff's face reddened.

Lauren rushed to her brother's aid. "All he meant, Mom, was that we're not kids anymore."

Donna and Travis considered the other two people at the table. When did this happen, they both thought. When did they grow up?

"That's a good point," Travis stated, looking first at Cliff, then Lauren. "And you're right, Cliff."

The boy looked up, surprised. "I am?"

Travis smiled. "Yes, Cliff. We sometimes forget that you're growing up..."

"...just like you sometimes forget to do your chores," Donna added, good-naturedly.

The boy reddened again, but smiled. "I get it."

"So, this summer is going to be different, right?" Lauren raised her milk glass in toast to the changing times.

"Yes," Donna confirmed, raising her wine glass. "To a better summer."

"A better summer," Travis agreed, raising his glass.

"Yeah," Cliff chimed in. "To a better summer."

Arnie P., who'd taken notice of the ebb and flow of the tone, had moved, unnoticed, to sit beside Travis' chair. As the toast came to an end, and the mood brightened, Arnie

P. joined the gaiety, barking his approval.

Travis reached down and lifted the small dog onto his lap.

"Well, it's official," Travis stated. "Even Arnie P. thinks it will be a better summer, don't ya, boy?"

The dog's stubby tail snapped excitedly from side to side. Two perfectly pitched barks were as pointed a response as was required.

"Exactly," Travis agreed, lowering the dog to the floor.

"So," Lauren asked, "if this is going to be a better summer, are you going to win the tournament this year?"

"Yeah, dad, are you going to kick Muck's..."

"Cliff!" Donna cut her son off before he could commit a punishable offense.

"I'm hopeful," Travis said, "but if today was any indication, this summer, so far as the golf goes, may be the same."

"What happened today?" Cliff looked expectantly to his father.

"Well," Travis began, taking a sip of his wine, "I played terribly and lost half my balls."

"Daddy," squealed Lauren, her eyes agog in terror. "That's gross!"

Cliff, now lost in a fit of pre-adolescent giggles, could only mutter the word 'balls' between breaths, which only reinforced the giggling.

"Golf balls," Travis corrected. "I lost half of my golf balls."

Donna glared at her husband. "I guess dinner's over."

* * * * *

Donna and Travis sat at the dinner table. The kids were gone, the dinner dishes sat untouched, and there was wine to finish.

"Who knew that one word would set them off so?"

"Your daughter is becoming a young woman and has an ever growing knowledge of human anatomy, not to mention an ever deepening suspicion of how all the bits fit together."

"And Cliff?"

"He's a male," Donna shrugged, sipping her wine. "Penises, breasts, and methane will be the sum total of what fascinates him until well into his eighties."

Travis laughed.

"So, how bad was it?" Donna poured the last of the wine into her husband's glass.

"Not good," he answered. "No matter what I did today turned bad. Losing the golf balls was the least of it, but the most obvious."

Donna nodded. No stranger to athletics or competition, she knew only too well what her husband was feeling. It was just a game, she knew, but that was never an excuse for doing less than your best. And if the best was, on any given day, less than anticipated, that only added to the frustration.

Of course, things might have been different if he'd bothered to wear his glasses.

He shook his head in wonder. "When did they get so big?"

She sipped her wine, looking through the doorway into the den where Lauren and Cliff were watching television. She'd been wondering the same thing herself.

"It was bound to happen," she answered.

"I know," he agreed, "but when? I was here the whole time. They were only babies...what...a few years ago?"

"It's been longer than that," she smiled.

"I know," he said, "about fourteen and eleven years, respectively."

"Kids grow up and get older."

He nodded. "And so do we, I guess."

"Speak for yourself, geezer," Donna huffed. "I'm still the hard bodied vixen you fell for all those years ago."

She's right, he acknowledged. Looking at her it was hard to see that the shapely, attractive woman sitting across from him was a forty-two year old mother of two. She still excited him.

"Yes," he agreed, smiling, "but you've sold your soul to the Devil for eternal youth, while I will grow old, die, and go to Heaven."

She smiled. "I don't know about that, but we are getting older."

And there it was. That was what his golf game had hinted at, and what their dinner conversation had crystallized.

"I guess you're right," he sighed. "When did we get so old?"

"Not old, honey." Donna moved to her husband. "Just older. You had a bad day on the course, and your vision isn't what it used to be. You need to start wearing your glasses. You have myopia, dear, which is a far cry from a retirement home or an ice floe."

Travis snorted. "Glasses." His success as a lawyer depended to a significant degree on appearances. Luckily, he hadn't needed them in court...yet. And his one attempt at using contacts had failed miserably. But this wasn't about his vision, he reminded himself, it was about finding really well hidden golf balls. What he needed was an enhanced sense of smell.

"And there's nothing we can do about the kids growing up. As long as we kept feeding them, it was bound to happen."

"We could quit feeding them?"

"You're the lawyer. Starving your children is still a crime, right?"

"Right."

She hugged him. "We've got a lot of years in front of us, so relax."

"You're right," he agreed, kissing her forehead.

"Of course, I'm right," she chided. "I'm your wife."

Arnie P. appeared in the kitchen doorway. He'd been off with the kids.

Travis smiled at the dog, who cocked his head. He was a good dog, Dempsey thought, thinking of all the joy he'd brought to the family.

"Why don't you go out back and practice your chip

shot," Donna suggested.

It was a good idea, he thought. It would relax him, and it certainly couldn't hurt his game. He'd need a better game once the tournament started.

"Hopefully I won't lose any golf balls." He smiled at the thought, but something was nagging at the back of his mind. A random thought from earlier.

"Take your glasses with you and stay out of my garden." She stepped away, noticing the terrier for the first time. "Take Arnie P., too. He can use the exercise."

The dog chuffed excitedly.

Travis smiled. He picked up the glasses from the kitchen counter where he'd left them earlier in the day. He stared at them as though they might sprout fangs and bite him.

The terrier chuffed again.

"I don't like them either," Dempsey admitted.

The dog raced his master to the back door.

* * * * *

It was a large back yard, befitting the large house it complemented. The house itself sat on a three-acre lot. On either side of the house were thin stands of trees, planted for privacy, though the Dempsey's nearest neighbors were fifty yards distant. The front of the house sat well back from the state road that ran from Stafford to Fredericksburg, and was where the school bus picked up the kids. The back of the house had a large deck that, itself, overlooked a stylish brick patio. Beyond that there was an expansive lawn, several gardens, open fields, and woods.

Dempsey dumped his golf paraphernalia on the lawn and donned his glasses. The distance suddenly became focused and crisp. These do make it easier to see, he admitted, understanding that losing balls might be less likely if he could actually follow the flight of the ball to its resting spot.

The weight on his nose, while slight, nagged at him,

reminding him of the presence of the glasses.

"So, whaddya think, Arnie?"

The dog, as unaccustomed to the glasses as his master, whimpered softly.

"I know," the man said, using his index finger to slide the glasses back in place. "They feel weird, too."

The dog chuffed.

It's not just the feeling, he thought. To be honest, it wasn't the feeling at all. It was the appearance. Even in his back yard he felt self-conscious, suddenly a high school freshman again with braces and a bad haircut.

Christ, he thought, I'm a successful lawyer with a wonderful wife, great kids, wealth, and financial security. I have what everyone strives for. Needing glasses shouldn't make a difference, should it?

Shouldn't, he conceded, but it does.

He pulled his pitching wedge from his bag and tossed a wiffle ball to the ground.

Dempsey settled over the ball, the head of his club resting in the grass just behind it. As he looked through the lenses, the ball was slightly blurred and appeared to be smaller. He turned his head and looked out towards the field. Clear as a bell. Looking back at the ball it was, again, blurred and distorted.

He tilted his head down, to peer over the top of the frames. As the ball came into focus, the glasses slid down his nose. He caught them before they fell from his face.

He pushed them back in place and tried addressing the ball again. Each time he was set to swing, he either lost sight of the ball, or the glasses shifted on his head.

Arnie P., head cocked in confusion, wondered what the holdup was.

Out of frustration, Dempsey finally just swung his club. The wedge dug a fine, long divot in the grass, and sent the ball dribbling a foot forward from its original spot.

If the dog could have laughed, he would have. He settled for a series of quick yaps.

Dempsey harrumphed and gave the dog a withering stare. It's not his fault, he told himself. If it weren't happening to me, I'd think it was funny, too.

He removed his glasses, looked at them as one might consider a two-headed salamander, and then tossed them to the side.

"Let's try this again," he said, resetting over the ball.

Arnie P., crouched forward with his rump in the air, waited excitedly for the ball to be hit. His eyes, round, brown circles of anticipation, alternated between his master's face and the ball resting in the grass.

As Dempsey swung his club, Arnie P. tensed, ready to spring into action. The club head hit the plastic ball with a distinctive 'tick', sending it skyward.

Much better, thought Dempsey.

The dog sprang forward, his small, muscular body springing across the yard, as his head, tracking the airborne white dot, remained steady and constant, never losing sight of his target.

The arc of the ball slowed, then stopped. Like a fatally wounded bird, it fell to the earth with all the grace and aerodynamic finesse of a rock.

And Arnie P. was there to meet it! Having anticipated the flight of the ball, the dog crouched in the grass a foot from where the plastic sphere landed. The game was that Arnie P. not touch the ball, but that he let the world know where it was, which he did with a series of rapid, staccato barks. In the short, neatly tended grass of the back yard, locating the ball was no challenge.

"Good job, boy," encouraged Dempsey, waggling the club in his hand. The swing was good, he thought, or seemed to be, so why was he pulling everything? He shook his head in disgust.

Arnie P. yelped excitedly.

"Okay. Bring it back."

The dog snatched the wiffle ball in his jaws and trotted proudly back to his master. He dropped the ball at Dempsey's feet, settling on his haunches and awaiting the praise he knew would be coming.

"What," teased Dempsey. "It's a wiffle ball. It's not like you dragged a caribou to the kitchen and started the oven."

The dog barked playfully, knowing that he was being teased.

"Now, if you could track down gold ingots," Dempsey muttered, winking at the dog, "that would be worth some serious doggy treats."

Arnie P. barked again, his tail whipped in excitement.

"Dare I say," whispered the man, looking around the yard to make certain he couldn't be overheard, "filet mignon?"

The dog barked again, taking a few tentative steps away, as if to tell his master to quit talking.

"I know," Dempsey said, "just hit the damn thing, right?"

Which he proceeded to do. He worked on his swing, making sure to keep his head down and follow through, while the terrier chased after his shots, never touching the balls until Dempsey gave the word.

As the sun began to set, the balls began to blur. He could see them clearly enough initially, but tended to lose them as they fell into shadow. Arnie P., however, was undaunted.

"If only I had your stamina," Dempsey muttered to his friend, "and your eyesight."

As he addressed the ball, his words replayed, and the nagging in the back of his mind slammed forward into his awareness.

He stepped to his bag and pulled out a regular golf ball.

"Let's give something a try, fella."

The dog cocked his head in anticipation of a new game.

Dempsey noted the markings on the ball, and then dropped it to the ground. He turned so that he'd be hitting the ball deep into the field of high grass behind the house.

He was about forty yards from the edge of the field, which started just beyond one of Donna's fenced in gardens.

His swing was slow and precise, and the ball sailed into the darkening sky and fell to earth just beyond the near edge of the field.

Arnie P. looked up at Dempsey, uncertainty showing in

his chocolate eyes.

"Well," Dempsey said, looking down at his small companion, "go see it you can find it."

The terrier looked out at the field, back at Dempsey, then back to the field. This was a new game, and he was uncertain how to proceed. His indecision didn't last long.

Like a rifle shot, Arnie P. flew across the manicured lawn, past the garden, and into the tall grass beyond.

Dempsey squinted, trying to keep track of the dog in the field, but the light, distance, and height of the grass conspired against him. It had been a foolish thought, he conceded. He looked at the glasses lying in the grass next to his bag. Resignation began to descend.

He was about to put the club back in the bag when excited barking issued from the field.

"Well, I'll be!" He raised his voice. "Bring it back, Arnie. Bring it back."

"What have you done with my dog?" Donna had come out to the deck to check on her husband.

"He's out in the field."

"What's he doing out there?"

"Finding golf balls."

Donna shook her head. "That's one nasty hook, honey."

Arnie P. emerged from the grass, strutting regally from the field. In his mouth was a white ball, which he dropped at Dempsey's feet.

It was the ball he'd hit into the field.

Dempsey smiled, the idea he had so quickly abandoned earlier now seemed to have a bit more merit.

"Maybe you should take up checkers," his wife offered helpfully from the deck. "Or wear your glasses, maybe?"

"Go back inside," Dempsey replied. "Arnie P. and I have work to do."

He hit the next ball deeper into the field. The Jack Russell charged off to find it.

"This," he muttered, "just might work."

JUNE

The Van Courtland Glen Country Club began life modestly; a simple, unchallenging eighteen holes nestled in the rolling hills of Spotsylvania County, Virginia. Envisioned back in the 1930s as a scenic getaway for weekend golfers, the original owner had set modest goals for a packet of land he'd picked up for a song.

Mercer Van Courtland, a native Virginian, had always loved golf, and lamented the paucity of playable courses available in the immediate Fredericksburg area, his hometown. Already in his mid-fifties, with money enough for twelve lifetimes, Van Courtland created the club for his own entertainment, trusting that, with time, the game would grow in stature, moving beyond its appearance as an entertaining diversion for the indolent rich, becoming a recreational pastime for the masses. Not everyone had agreed with Van Courtland's assessment, but few argued the logic of buying up thousands of acres of gently rolling land to build on. The course could expand over time, he'd reasoned, and if not, he could always sell the land later at a profit. It had never come to that. With time came ideas, and with ideas had come investors. Mostly, though, time had brought Mercer Van Courtland to the realization that *his* time was coming to a close, and if he wanted to leave some mark on the world, he'd better get started.

Design and construction of the expanded Van

Courtland Glen County Club had begun in 1953. Upgrades to the original course were planned, along with the construction of three additional, eighteen-hole courses. Each course was oriented on one of the major compass points, with each course named for its particular point of orientation. The one exception to this had been the South Course. As the original course, it was known alternately as either the South Course or, to those in the know, The Old Course.

The hub of the compass was the Course Estate, a huge, rambling fifty thousand square foot clubhouse containing banquet facilities, two pro shops, and a number of bars, dining rooms, locker rooms, and maintenance shops. There were even a half dozen efficiency apartments tucked away on the top floor of the grand, colonial style building. The rooms typically remained empty, but because the Course Estate had evolved into a conference center, the small apartments were sometimes pressed into service as meeting rooms. By and large, though, the club was all about golf.

It was a private club, but non-members were welcome, as long as they played with a member. Even so, they were only allowed to play the Old Course and the West Course. The North and East Courses, by far the best, most challenging of the four, were reserved exclusively for members, though the members had access to all four courses.

The club also had two driving ranges, one between the Old and West Courses, the other between the North and East Courses, along with large ball machines to dispense buckets of range balls. Cart farms and pro shops were situated near each range, facilitating warm-up and the timely start of each round. And timeliness was very important to the man charged with overseeing the day-to-day operation of the course, as well as at the annual tournament.

"Rounds will move at a brisk pace," said the man in the dark green tartan kilt, his tam-o'-shanter, the same green tartan, tilted carefully forward on his head. "If ya slow down, the marshal will give ya a prod. If ya ignore the marshal, you'll be dealin' with me."

McTavish was an old, weathered Scot, his wrinkled face a detailed relief map of a life lived outdoors. Though he'd lived in the United States for more than half of his sixty years, his Highland brogue was as thick as the porridge he'd grown up on, and as incomprehensible to some as the notion that a real man would willingly, proudly, wear a skirt. His native attire aside, no one ever questioned the short, sturdy man when it came to golf. As the Starter of the Courses, he was the golfer's loving and vengeful god, the final word on all things golf at Van Courtland Glen's four courses. His word was law on the links, and not even the richest, most powerful member would think to challenge McTavish.

The Scot loved and revered the game, a passion developed in youth that had grown with him into adulthood. He understood that not everyone shared his reverence for the game, but he was adamant that anyone playing the game would, at the very least, respect its spirit. It was a proper, dignified game, played by the dignified and well mannered, and if an individual couldn't honor the sport by maintaining a modicum of civility for a modest few hours, that individual would be sent packing. "The game will be honored," he'd been heard to say on more than one occasion, "even if there's nane left to play it."

It was early morning, the Sunday before Memorial Day. The short, thickset Scot was at the front of the club's main banquet hall. Behind him, on the wall, was a large map of the Van Courtland Glen Country Club. Flanking McTavish were a number of stern looking men in blood red jackets and white ball caps. Printed across the front of each cap, in bold black letters, was the word 'Marshal', just to make certain there would be no confusion as to who had the upper hand on the course.

The room was filled to capacity with men and women dressed in casual golf clothing. No one wore shorts or skirts...club rules forbid such clothing until much later in the summer...but there were plenty of colorful, garish shirts, slacks, and caps, enough to keep the fashion world scratching their collective heads for years to come.

The attendees sat quietly at their tables, reviewing their tournament packages, as McTavish explained, as he did every year, the tournament rules.

"The ladies will play from the red tees, the men from the whites." The dour Scot, his deep, rich voice filling the room, paced in front of the golfers, his leather sporran swaying gently as he moved. "There are no exceptions, so you would-be pros rein in your egos and play with the mortals."

Light, nervous laughter rippled through the crowd.

"Each team is made up of four players, members only. Where fewer than four registered for a team, we assigned singles as we thought best. If you've been assigned to a group you can't stand, or a player assigned to your group is a cousin from your spouse's side of the family, or just a wanker, see me before the rounds begin. We'll do what we can to keep everyone happy and avoid bloodshed."

Weak applause rattled from the back of the room.

"Each team must play as a team. There will be no substitutions allowed. In the event of the death or incapacitation of one of the team members, the entire team is disqualified."

The room was as quiet as a crypt.

"To those who are new to our tournament, this is not a new rule nor, to our way of thinking, a harsh one. At the very least, the rule protects the life of the weakest member of the foursome. We'll not have a replay of the 1984 fiasco!"

Applause and laughter brought McTavish to a stop. He waited for the room to settle before resuming.

"Today's round and the final round are the only set rounds of play for the tournament, and are the only days on which we dictate which course each team will play. Each team will play a total of fourteen rounds. Discounting the opening round and the closing round, that leaves twelve rounds. Any team that doesn't record a total of fourteen rounds, for whatever reason, will be disqualified.

"Each team is required to play each of the four courses three times between now and Labor Day weekend, the tournament period, exclusive of the opening and closing rounds. Before each round, the team must declare if they are playing a tournament round. You'll find the declaration forms in your folders."

The sound of papers rustling filled the room.

"If you don't declare a tournament round before the first drive, the round will not count. At the conclusion of a declared round of play, each team will turn in a signed and witnessed scorecard. Scorecards must be submitted to the tournament office in the north pro shop within thirty minutes of the completion of the round. No late cards will be accepted."

McTavish smiled wickedly at the crowd.

"But more on that later." The Scot cleared his throat. "Are there any questions so far?"

There never were. He nodded and continued.

"The highest score a player can get per hole is three over par. A triple bogey is the highest that will be recorded. There will also be no 'mulligans,'" he snorted derisively, "nor will there be any 'gimme' putts. Each stroke is recorded. If you have your triple before you finish the hole, pick your ball up and move on. As I said, play will move briskly.

"Scoring will be calculated as follows. Each player on each team will have his or her own score for the round. At the end of the round, the four scores will be added together, then divided by four, giving an average team score for the round. After all fourteen rounds have been played, the highest and lowest team scores will be thrown out and the remaining scores will be added together, then divided by twelve, taking into account each player's handicap, resulting in an average team score for the tournament. It is that final score that will determine the winner."

McTavish paused, sweeping the room with his steely gaze. All eyes were on him, waiting for him to continue.

"Lost score cards are a problem every year, but we

handle them as we always have. The first time a team loses a card, that round will count as their best round throwaway score. The second lost card will count as the team's worst round throwaway score. A third lost card disqualifies the team.

"As for late submissions of cards to the tournament office, they will be treated as lost cards. The first late submission will be treated like the first lost card." He smiled at the crowd. "I think you can figure out the rest."

McTavish straightened himself and clasped his hands behind his back. Chest jutted commandingly forward, he beamed over the crowd.

"As always, all course rules will be observed by all players. If you have a question, ask a referee. If you don't like the answer, ask me. And if you don't like my answer," he said, rocking forward on the balls of his feet, "you'll need to find another course to play."

The Scot was not surprised by the muttering that filled the room. It always happened. He didn't lord his authority over these folks, most of who had more money than any hundred Scots back home, but he took his job seriously. He was paid to ensure that the Van Courtland Glen Golf Course ran smoothly, and that the courses achieved and maintained a reputation for quality play and superior playing conditions. He could do it, he knew, but only when the rules were followed. He was all too aware that some in the audience bridled at authority, especially from someone they deemed beneath them, but there was nothing to be done for it. As long as the President of the Club retained his services, he would continue to do his job, regardless of the toes stepped on or the feelings that were hurt. His job required it, and the sport demanded it.

"Be sure to check the boards in the pro shops for announcements and standings." He took in the expectant faces around him and smiled. "Good luck."

* * * * *

They were standing near the starter's booth for the West Course. Dempsey stood behind McTavish. Arnie P. sat quietly at his master's feet, peering up at the two men expectantly.

"Well," the Starter of the Courses said, wetting his finger and turning to the next page of the leather bound USGA rule book, "I've got to give you points for originality."

Dempsey shook his head. "Don't misunderstand me, McTavish. I'm not trying to pull a fast one. It's just that I could use a little help when my shots go missing."

"Couldn't we all," the Scot agreed, turning to another page. His tortoise shell reading glasses were perched dangerously close to the end of his slender nose. "Still, it is an odd request."

"Spoken with a Caledonian's gift of understatement."

McTavish snorted proudly, though he never came close to smiling. He turned another page.

Ten minutes passed in silence as McTavish consulted his bible. The tournament was getting underway, with the teams disbursing to their starting holes. The excitement in the golfers was palpable, a charge in the air that tickled the hair on the back of the neck and rubbed the stomach playfully.

As McTavish reviewed the rules, Dempsey stood quietly behind the man. For his part, Arnie P. didn't move. He watched the old Scot as though doggie treats might mysteriously, miraculously pour forth from beneath his tam.

McTavish closed his book and tucked it back into his sporran. He turned to face the other man. "Well, sir, you've bested the greatest golfing minds in the world."

"Not my intent," Dempsey assured him.

"I'm certain of that, Mr. Dempsey. Still, I wonder if I won't be opening a Pandora's Box."

"If it's going to cause you problems, don't worry about it."

"I'm not worried, Mr. Dempsey," McTavish stated. His eyes betrayed an active mind at work. He winked at the lawyer. "When you speak with the authority of God, there is little you need worry about."

Dempsey laughed.

"No," the starter continued, "I'm just wondering what happens if this works."

"If it works?"

"Maybe I should say if it works too well."

Dempsey shook his head.

"There is nothing so dangerous as the unanticipated success of an ill-conceived plan."

Dempsey's confusion was evident on his face.

"It tends to breed further stupidity," McTavish clarified.

Dempsey nodded, then gave Arnie P. a smile.

"Well, sport," the lawyer said to the dog, "looks like we'll have to give this a try another time."

"Not at all, Mr. Dempsey."

Travis gave the Scot a confused look. "But I thought…"

"We won't know a thing unless we try, will we?"

"I guess not."

McTavish addressed himself to Arnie P. "Are you up for this, laddie?"

The Jack Russell barked twice, barely able to contain his excitement.

"Good." The Scot turned his attention back to Dempsey. "Though there's nothing in the rules specifically, I believe we can get cream from this cow."

The Scot scratched his chin in thought as Dempsey wondered what the man had meant.

"He can be neither observer nor outside agency," the man mused, confirming his assessment with a nod. "He might qualify as equipment, thought that would be pushing it, don't you think?"

Dempsey tried to give the impression that he understood where the other man was going, but settled for a mute nod.

"So the best thing is to have him attend as a caddie."

"A caddie?"

The Scot nodded, and smiled. "With some modifications, of course."

The lawyer nodded.

"If he touches the ball in any way while in play, you'll be

taking a stroke."

Dempsey nodded again.

"If he makes a nuisance of himself, we'll need to put an end to this experiment immediately."

"Absolutely."

"And if I find any of his shite on the course, he'll be barred from further play..."

"...I understand..."

"...as will you..."

"...but..."

McTavish waved the other man to silence.

"It's nothing personal against you or the dog, Mr. Dempsey. Given the amount of goose crap on the course from our winged Canadian friends, it's a wonder anyone can play sometimes, especially in the fall. But people are funny that way, Mr. Dempsey. They'll gladly play a shot standing ankle deep in goose goo and not give it a second thought, but I'm going to hear about a ball that comes to rest next to a dog turd. People can question my decision to let your friend spot balls for you. Not much different than a caddie in that regards. But when a caddie starts leaving stinkers on the fairway, I have no easy way out."

The lawyer considered what the other man had said, not certain that he'd understood it all through the brogue. The gist of it, however, was clear.

"If you find any dog shit out on the course, Mac, it won't be from Arnie P. I give you my word."

"And I'll hold you to it."

The two men shook hands.

"Have a good starting round, Mr. Dempsey," the starter offered. He looked up at the lightening sky. Not a cloud in sight. "You have a grand day for it."

"Thank you."

McTavish lowered his voice conspiratorially.

"And Mr. Dempsey?"

"Yes?"

"If your caddie can help your team beat Muck, there'll be a steak dinner in it for him."

The Starter of the Courses bid the man and his dog

good morning and walked purposefully towards the clubhouse.

"You hear that," Dempsey said, giving Arnie P. the eye. "We beat Muck and McTavish is buying you dinner."

Arnie P. barked happily.

"Just don't touch anything," he said, turning towards his team, "and don't take a dump unless I know about it."

* * * * *

"This is an interesting turn of events," declared Pearsall. He sat in the passenger's seat of the golf cart. Sitting next to him on the seat was Arnie P. The lawyer and the terrier stared curiously at each other.

"Yeah," Verdu concurred, standing next to the cart. "Tell us again why Arnie P. is here?"

Dempsey cinched his golf bag snuggly into place on the back of the cart. They were running late and he was hustling to make up the time.

Clawson sat in the driver's seat of the second cart, hunched over the wheel.

"I'd be interested in hearing the story again," the man stated, his southern twang biting a bit more deeply in the morning cool.

"It's not a big deal," Dempsey assured them, pulling balls, tees, and a glove from his bag. "Arnie's going to make sure I don't lose any balls today."

"Given that you persuaded McTavish that this was a good idea," Clawson observed, "I'd say you've got balls to spare."

"Very funny."

"It is odd," Verdu said. He checked his watch. "But we'll have to worry about this later. We've got about four minutes to get to the fifth tee."

Dempsey climbed into the cart. "Let's go, then."

"Are you sure about this," Pearsall wondered, giving the dog a troubled look. "I mean, golfing and seeing-eye dogs are not a logical mix. At least, not for me."

"He's not a seeing-eye dog," Dempsey protested. He patted the dog lovingly on the head. "He's a highly trained ball spotter. There is nowhere on this course where any of our shots, no matter how badly struck, will be able to hide. If a ball lands in the fairway and we can see it, Arnie P. sits in the cart. If a ball goes missing, Arnie P. will be pressed into service."

"Right."

"Hell, if we play well, Arnie P. may not need to get out of the cart."

Pearsall gave his law partner a withering look. "I'm certain we'll all play like pros today."

"Let's go," Clawson yelled.

Arnie P. gave the black man with the bald head and the colorful Hawaiian shirt one last look, then turned his attention forward. As though in agreement with Clawson, the dog barked excitedly.

"It's going to be fine, Mitch. You won't even know he's here."

Dempsey steered the cart towards the fifth hole. He was hoping he hadn't done something stupid. It was unlikely. Or, as Donna had said to him when he'd laid out his plan: "It is stupid, honey. But it's not fatal." A real comfort, that wife of his, but she was probably right. The worst that could happen was that Arnie P. wouldn't be able to find any balls, or that he'd nudge them with his snout. And then he remembered McTavish's admonishment.

"Just let me know if you see him taking a dump somewhere, okay?"

Pearsall looked at his friend in shock and disbelief.

* * * * *

The first three holes went off without a hitch. Though Dempsey couldn't follow his shots much past a hundred and fifty yards...the fast departing white sphere blended nicely with the gray/blue of the morning sky...Clawson or Verdu could follow his drives clearly enough to spot where

31

they'd landed. Arnie P. stayed in the cart, under the watchful eye of Pearsall.

"He keeps staring at me," he would announce to no one in particular. "It's freakin' me out."

"Christ, Mitch," Clawson laughed. "You spend your days with killers, thieves, and other lawyers. Certainly a cute little mutt like Arnie isn't a threat."

On number eight, a par five, five hundred and twenty yard dogleg to the right, Verdu sent his drive down the center of the fairway, keeping the trees on the left and the thick grass to the right out of play. His drive bounced down the fairway and came to rest just as the fairway began its turn.

"Sweet," the small man stated. He picked up his tee and strutted over to his friends. He nodded to Clawson. "Match that…if you can."

"You don't leave a man much to work with, Vince."

Clawson set his ball, looked down the fairway, and addressed the ball. He took a slow, easy back swing, then released. The distinctive 'crack' of driver striking ball, at the center of the sweet spot, rang out. The ball rose fast and true into the air, fading gently right as it hit the apex of its arc. As it fell it continued its gradual drift to the right, easily making the turn and leaving Verdu's ball some twenty yards in its wake.

"You bastard," Verdu smiled. Pearsall and Dempsey laughed good-naturedly. "That was beautiful."

Clawson tipped his hat appreciatively. "The benefit of a pampered youth."

Dempsey stepped up to the white tee markers. "If we keep playing like this," he said, teeing his ball, "we'll bury Muck by the 4th of July."

He settled into his stance and addressed the ball. His swing was smooth, and his drive went as straight as an arrow.

Being a bigger hitter than Vince, and less skilled in shaping a shot than Clawson, Dempsey's drive sailed past Verdu's, past the turn, and bounded towards the trees on the far end of the fairway turn.

"Oh, no," he muttered. He hadn't seen where it ended up, but he could tell that he'd hit it cleanly.

"You got all of it," Pearsall confirmed, stepping up to drive.

"I don't think you made the woods," stated Verdu, "but you overdrove the fairway."

Clawson smiled. "If this was a straight par five, you'd be in prime shape to make the green in two."

"If it had been a straight fairway," Dempsey said, snatching his tee from the ground and getting out of Pearsall's way, "I would have hooked the bastard."

The Southerner shrugged knowingly. The game was the game.

Pearsall addressed his ball. A nice, easy swing, he told himself. Don't swing too hard, he thought. Let the club do the work. He pictured himself taking the club back slowly, deliberately, focusing on the ball as his muscle memory turned his torso ever so slightly. He imagined his body turned, left arm back across his chest, the right arm bent at the elbow, with the head of the driver just visible is his left periphery. In his mind he saw himself bring his driver around in a smooth, balanced arch, pulling the club through the swing with his left hand, not pushing with his right, turning his hips and snapping his wrists a fraction of a second before striking the ball. The action was followed by the cannon report of his club head hitting the ball, continuing the swing and following through as the ball, a clear, white dot, shot forward, fading right like Clawson's drive, but besting his friends shot by ten yards.

In his internal world, where he worked to pattern his golf success, his friends fell over themselves to congratulate him for what was, he was certain, the most amazing drive any of them had ever seen. Even Arnie P. was impressed.

Pearsall took a deep breath, looked down the fairway and picked his target. He returned his gaze to the ball on the tee in front of him. Slowly, as he'd imagined it, he began his back swing. It was the only part of his swing that remotely mirrored his intent.

The back swing was too fast, and his arms were all wrong. His torso turned too much, which forced his swing to rush, pushed through the swing by his right hand. As the club met the ball, his balance shifted unexpectedly, forcing him to fall back off the drive. Sensing just how badly his plans had turned, his head came up too soon, hoping to catch a glimpse of what he could only hope was a shot that didn't kill one of his friends.

The ball jumped skyward, moving forward at what seemed, initially, to be a calculated fade. Almost immediately, though, the ball appeared to be taken by a gale force wind, slammed further to the right, turning the fade into a killer slice.

"Uh-oh," Vince croaked.

The errant ball continued its rightward course unabated.

"We can just wait here," Clawson observed, eyeing the ball carefully. "Looks like it's on its way back."

As the four watched, the ball fell into the high grass to the right of the fairway. There was no bounce. The ball went into the grass and vanished.

"Well," Pearsall said, looking disgustedly at the expanse of deep, thick green, "that wasn't quite what I had in mind."

"That goes without saying," agreed Clawson, "though it was an amazing shot."

"Yeah," Dempsey echoed. "It looked as though you set up fine..."

"...and then your central nervous system convulsed," finished Verdu.

Pearsall nodded, not taking his buddies comments personally. The smallest of details, the most insignificant of shifts in the grip or stance, tended to have a major impact on a player's swing.

"It felt fine," he commented, "until I started the swing."

The three other men nodded, each understanding that, once the swing began, the commitment was made.

"Well," Clawson said, moving to the cart, "let's go find it."

"Yeah," Verdu agreed. "We only have five minutes."

Dempsey stood his ground, staring at the small, excited rider in the cart. Arnie P. sat on the seat, though his rump twitched excitedly, barely contained energy waiting to be released. His ears were cocked forward. His eyes were riveted to the field of grass to the right of the fairway. His mouth was open slightly, almost in a smile.

Pearsall looked at his law partner, then at the Jack Russell.

"Give me your glove, Mitch." Dempsey held out his hand.

"You're joking, right?"

Dempsey didn't answer. Slowly, Pearsall removed his glove and handed it to his friend.

With glove in hand, Dempsey went to the cart and waved the glove under Arnie P.'s nose.

"This is it, Arnie," the man whispered. "You know what to do, so go and do it, okay?"

The dog looked excitedly at his master. At Dempsey's nod, the small dog leapt from the cart and charged down the fairway.

"This has got to be the weirdest thing I've ever seen," Clawson said.

Verdu looked around nervously. "I just hope no one sees us."

"Quit jawin', boys," Dempsey said. "We've got a ball to find."

"But I thought..." Pearsall climbed into the cart.

"He should be able to find the ball," Dempsey agreed, climbing behind the wheel. "But a little of our help couldn't hurt."

The two carts sped after the dog, angling towards the edge of the fairway. As they neared the spot where the ball had fallen, they parked the carts.

"Where'd he go?" Verdu stood on the edge of the fairway, scanning the tall green of the field.

"Arnie?" Dempsey called out. There was no response.

Clawson grabbed a club from his bag and began searching. "C'mon, guys. Times a wastin'."

The four men began searching through the grass, swatting the think tufts of green with their clubs.

"Are you sure this was the spot," asked Pearsall. He looked back to the tee box, trying to gauge the flight of the ball to determine where it would have landed.

"This is the spot," Clawson confirmed, shaking his head in disgust. "Trouble is, there are rocks everywhere." As if to prove his point, his club head clanked into a large, rough edged chunk of stone. "Your ball could have gone anywhere. There's just no way to tell."

Pearsall muttered angrily under his breath. Reaching into his pocket, he pulled out another ball. He was ready to take a drop when Arnie P. began barking.

He was fifteen yards nearer the green, and though the men couldn't see him clearly, they could just make out an animated patch of white and brown in a field of green.

They walked towards the Jack Russell. He stood three feet away from a golf ball that had settled a foot from the edge of the first cut. It rested on a small patch of short grass, a small island clearing within the thick, unforgiving thatch.

"Ah, shit," Dempsey sputtered. "He must have moved it."

"Why do you say that?" Clawson stepped up to the ball and looked at the ground around it.

"Look at it. What are the odds that it would land sitting up like that."

"I don't know what the odds are," Clawson said, "but I know something about tracking, and your dog hasn't touched that ball."

"You can tell that just by looking?" Verdu was impressed, learning yet another useful tidbit of information about their friend from the South.

Clawson nodded. "The grass is undisturbed, except from over here, where the ball came from." He pointed off to where they'd been looking. "It must have hit a rock, ricocheted this way, and settled."

"If that's Mitch's ball."

It was a possibility they hadn't considered.

Pearsall leaned over and examined the ball, careful not to disturb the bed of grass. It was his, all right, the white orb now sporting a nasty scuff where it had contacted the rock.

He looked down at the dog sitting a few feet away. The small animal's shoulders were thrown back proudly.

"Amazing." Pearsall reached down and cautiously patted the dog's head. Arnie's eye's fluttered happily with each touch. "Simply amazing."

Pearsall removed his cap, placing it next to the ball.

The men returned to their carts with Arnie P. close on their heels, a magisterial bounce in his step. He jumped into the cart and settled on the seat between Dempsey and Pearsall. The tall black man carefully rested his hand on the dog's back, giving the Jack Russell a gentle rub.

* * * * *

The ninth hole was a straight par four with a wide-open fairway that narrowed towards the green, funneling all the shots toward the pin. With good drives and respectable second shots, the Dempsey foursome ended their first five holes at one under par.

On their way to the 10th, they stopped at the clubhouse to give Mitch a chance to use the restrooms. Their moods were bright and buoyant. Even Arnie P., whose services had been used only once, appeared optimistic that there were big things in store for all of them.

"There's not a reason in the world we shouldn't feel good about our play," Dempsey agreed. He stayed in the cart as Pearsall scooted into the clubhouse.

"Man's got a bladder the size of a bottle cap," observed Verdu, just loudly enough for Pearsall to hear. Without looking back, the tall man shot Verdu the bird.

Clawson laughed. He stepped from his cart and went over to Dempsey's. Verdu joined them. Arnie P. barked his greeting.

"You are one talented mutt," Verdu said, patting the terrier's head. "I'm looking forward to great things from you."

The dog chuffed excitedly, as though to assure Verdu that he'd hold up his end of the deal.

"Yeah," Clawson agreed. "With Arnie's help, we might just end up takin' the whole ball of wax."

"It's a very large ball of wax," a deep, growling voice rumbled behind them. "And I think we'll have something to say about it."

The speaker was a large, bear-like man with a barrel chest, crew cut, and lantern jaw. He was flanked by three men of various shapes and heights, but it was clear that he was their leader.

Dempsey, Clawson, and Verdu turned as one to see the ursine man glowering down at them. Arnie P. looked quickly over his shoulder, then just as quickly looked away. His small body began to tremble. Dempsey reached out and calmed the dog.

"Well, if it isn't Mr. Muck and his golfing buddies," Clawson declared, "Baxter, Pfunke, and Howe. I was wondering when our paths would cross."

"Wonder no longer, cornpone," Muck said, flashing the Southerner a set of teeth that looked out of place without a struggling salmon between them. "We were just making the turn and thought we'd say 'hi.'"

"That was very thoughtful," Verdu observed. The large man nodded grandly. "And totally out of character."

Muck eyed the short, muscular man critically. The tension in the air was thick and growing.

No one was clear on where or when the animosity between the two groups first began, and it was likely that none of the men involved remembered what had first sparked what had become a legendary Van Courtland Glen course rivalry. In all likelihood the rift had occurred over an unfortunate choice of words, or an innocent misunderstanding, some trivial event that, with any other mix of personalities, would have dissipated like a thin ground fog on a warm spring morning.

But the fog had never cleared.

Some speculated that the reason for the open

animosity between the two groups stemmed from some serious breach of etiquette that had occurred away from the club. An affair, perhaps, or a business deal gone bad, something that made reconciliation unlikely, if not impossible. Others had a less complex assessment of the situation; some folks just didn't hit it off, no matter what, and it was just a matter of time before the people involved saw no more value in the charade of civility. And where most club members steered clear of Muck, certainly when he was with his buddies, and most assuredly during the annual golf tournament, Dempsey, Pearsall, Verdu, and Clawson were not the least bit intimidated by Muck, Jauncy Baxter, Barnibus Pfunke, and Charles Howe.

"So you guys are going to try to win the tournament?" Charles Howe was a man of medium height and medium build. Generally non-descript in every way possible, people seemed to notice him only when he was with the other three, and that was the only time he felt brave enough to speak up. "Again?"

Muck and the others laughed, an angry sound that sent starlings in a nearby tree noisily skyward.

"Careful, Chuck." Dempsey looked up and met Howe's non-descript gray eyes. "Keep making jokes like that and people might think you're developing a personality."

Clawson snorted. "No danger of that, is there, Chuck?"

"It's Charles," Howe stated, testily. "Don't call me Chuck."

"Now, don't get your knickers in a twist, Chuck." Verdu stepped forward. He was in no way threatening, but his muscled, bullish frame sent a clear message. "It's all in good fun. Hell," he said, pointing to Clawson, "I'm golfing with cornpone, remember?"

"That's *Mister* Cornpone to you, Vince." Clawson warned his friend good-naturedly. Without missing a beat, the Southerner winked at Howe. "But you can call me Poonie, Chuck."

"It's Charles," Howe insisted, his face reddening. His hands slowly curled into fists. "Don't call me Chuck."

"Right," Dempsey acknowledged. The sport of it, by

39

unspoken understanding, was to push the others, not trip them. It was obvious to Dempsey that Howe's fuse was much shorter than normal today, which gave him an idea.

"So, Charles, how's your game going?"

Before the non-descript man could answer, Muck jumped in.

"We're playing better this year than last," he crowed. His chest swelled in pride. "Hell, we keep playing like this and we'll have the cup sewn up by late July."

It was bluster, of course, and everyone knew it, including Muck.

Dempsey smiled. "End of July, eh?"

"I'm just saying," Muck began. His usual, cocksure expression faltered slightly. He sensed that he'd overplayed his hand. "It could happen."

"I've got some money that says you won't have it wrapped up by then." Clawson, following Dempsey's lead, stepped over to stand closer to Muck. He wanted to watch the man's expression more closely.

"How much?" Barnibus Pfunke was a short, spindly man, somewhere in his mid-forties. At first blush he looked to be frail, but he was fairly fast and aggressive. His forcefulness always took people by surprise, but one look at his toupee made people quickly forget everything else about the man.

"I don't know," shrugged Clawson. "Somebody make me an offer."

"That's not fair," Howe protested. "Poonie's got more money than God..."

"...and certainly more than all of us put together."

Jauncy Baxter was an Adonis-like man whose frame, facial features, hair, voice, gate, and overall appearance blended together into the perfect package. He was, by anyone's estimation, a gorgeous man, and the only person more beautiful than him was his wife, Elizabeth. But what Jauncy possessed in looks he lacked in substance. He was a man with no intelligence, no sense, and no reason to think that he needed either. God had been looking out for Jauncy, making sure that he was born into a wealthy family, because he would never have survived in the real world on his own.

"Well," Verdu asked, "if not money, what?"

"I know," Dempsey said, stepping out of the cart and standing in front of Muck. "How about this. If you guys don't have the tournament sewn up by the end of July, you drop out."

"Of the tournament?" Baxter couldn't quite grasp the concept.

"We could do that," Howe acknowledged, turning a questioning look to Muck, "couldn't we, T.J.?"

Muck's smile was cold and passionless. "We could," he confirmed, "but why would we?"

"Because you would want to back up your braggadocio with action?"

"It's a good try, Travis," Muck said, "but we're in it for the duration."

"I thought you would be," Dempsey stated, choosing not to pursue the issue any further. "A real pity, though."

"Yeah," agreed Verdu. "You guys could show some real class and character with a move like that."

Baxter snorted derisively. "We're not about class and character. We're about winning."

"That's what I've always said about you, Jauncy." Clawson smiled knowingly at his friends. "You are just a pretty face."

The handsome man brightened. "You mean it?"

"I've never been more sincere in all my life."

"Baxter, you idiot," Muck hissed, "the man just called you stupid."

"He's got me there, Jauncy," Clawson confessed, "but I really was sincere about your good looks."

Confused, Baxter wandered off to his cart.

"What's with the mutt?" Muck looked down at Arnie P. The dog looked at the ursine man from the corner of his eye.

"He's helping us play," Verdu offered, only too late realizing that the less Muck knew, the better.

"Oh?"

"He's along for the ride. That's all." Dempsey tried to distract Muck, but he could tell that the other man was intrigued by the appearance of a dog where there shouldn't be one.

"Baby sitting, eh?" Muck leaned into the cart and reached out to pet Arnie P. The dog caught the motion out of the corner of his eye. He growled softly, turned, and snapped at the beefy hand reaching for him.

The big man snatched his hand away quickly.

"Nasty little fuck, isn't he." Muck checked his hand. "Lucky he didn't bite me, Dempsey."

"Poor thing would need shots," Clawson mumbled. Only Verdu heard the comment, but his soft laugh drew the bearish man's attention.

"I say something funny," Muck growled.

Verdu shook his head, but couldn't quite get the smile off his face.

"Sorry about that, T.J." Dempsey shot Arnie P. a stern look. "Bad dog!"

"Yeah, well, no harm done, I guess." Muck's eyes never left the dog. "Just keep him out of my way."

"Not a problem," Dempsey assured the man. "And good luck."

Muck gave Dempsey and his friends a condescending look.

"Luck?" Muck sneered and walked away, Howe and Pfunke following in his wake.

"A lovely man," Clawson commented.

"A prince," Verdu observed.

Pearsall appeared from the clubhouse. "Was that Muck and his buddies?"

Dempsey nodded.

"Did anybody think to tell Pfunke that he's got a dead monkey on his head?"

Verdu laughed, Clawson smiled, and Dempsey just rolled his eyes. The only one who cared to comment was Arnie P. He barked excitely at the return of his tall friend.

Pearsall eyed the dog thoughtfully. "You ready to play?"

"He's about to become history," Dempsey warned, "if he doesn't behave."

"What did he do?"

"He almost bit Muck."

"Really?"

Verdu nodded seriously.

Pearsall beamed. "Good boy." He climbed into the cart and gave the pooch a pat. Arnie P. reciprocated by excitedly licking the big man's hand. "Next time," coached Pearsall, "lean in a bit closer so you won't miss."

"That's right, Mitch. Encourage him."

"He knew what he wanted to do," Pearsall countered. "He just didn't execute."

Dempsey settled into the cart, shaking his head.

*　*　*　*　*

The first day of Van Courtland Glen Country Club's annual tournament went off flawlessly. Even the weather, unpredictable in the late spring, remained clear and calm the entire day. It was *the* perfect day for golf.

Dempsey, Pearsall, Verdu, and Clawson slowly but surely improved their game. With each additional hole their confidence grew, but it wasn't all smooth sailing.

On fourteen, a straight par three that dropped from the tee box to the green, and was surrounded on three sides by trees, Verdu hit his drive fat, sending the ball rocketing across the green, one hundred and twenty three yards away, and into the stand of trees behind the pin. Arnie P. was able to find the ball quickly, and though the lie was miserable, Verdu was able to salvage a scrambling bogey.

Eighteen proved a bit of a challenge to the foursome. A long par four, the fairway eased to the right around some trees, and from the tees the players could just see the left edge of the green. The ideal shot would place the drive slightly right of center in the fairway. With trees on the right, and a grassy hill on the left as the fairway turned, there was little room for error.

Pearsall's drive ended up in perfect position, effectively cutting the corner of the fairway and leaving his way clear to the green. Verdu's drive, while not as good, still left him in the fairway on the far side. A longer second shot, but straight and clear to the pin. It was Clawson and Dempsey who got in trouble with their drives.

In trying to cut the corner, Clawson's drive went from the desired fade to a serious slice shortly after leaving the tee. Had it simply gone into the trees on the right, there wouldn't have been a problem. But as they'd watched the shot sail into the woods, they heard the distinctive 'pock' of the ball hitting tree limbs.

"Anybody see where it landed?"

No one could answer Clawson's question.

Unlike Clawson, Dempsey tried only for the fairway. Any part of the fairway. In easily the best drive of his life, he cannoned his drive as straight as an artillery shell down the fairway...and beyond. His ball came to rest in the deep grass on the distant hill.

Arnie P., sitting at the side of the tee box, stared forward, eyes shifting from left to right, ears cocked forward. With a nod from Dempsey, the Jack Russell sprinted towards the woods, followed by Verdu and Clawson in their cart.

The dog was a whirlwind of activity, a white and brown blur of concentrated, ball hunting fury. After five minutes, neither dog nor golfers could find Clawson's ball.

"That's bad luck," Clawson stated. "That costs me a stroke."

"What?"

"Lost ball or out of bounds. Either way, it's a stroke." Clawson pointed to the white stakes at the edge of the woods. The Southerner looked down at the terrier sitting next to him. "Not your fault, Arnie. Go help the others. Go on."

The small dog had better luck with Dempsey's ball. The ball hit and rolled under the grass on the hill. Once under the heavy grass, however, the ball rolled along a dried runnel that carried it about forty feet downhill from where it had originally hit, and from where Dempsey and Pearsall had been looking.

Almost instantly, Arnie P. located the ball and called attention to his find. It hadn't been a great lie, but it was preferable to trying to hit off the slope of the hill.

By the time the foursome finished their round, Arnie P. had earned his keep. Even Clawson, a man who owned a half dozen parrots and was generally neutral on dogs, felt a certain affection for the wiry little quadruped.

"You're okay, Arnie," he said, reaching down to pet the dog. "Don't know that my parrots would think so, but they're just birds."

The dog responded with an excited chuff.

Dempsey stepped from the cart with the scorecard.

"Okay," he began, "here's how we did today."

The others gathered around Dempsey. Arnie P. settled in at his master's feet.

"Rex, you played a seventy-nine. That penalty hurt, but still good. Vince, you managed an eighty-three. So did I. Mitch, with an eighty-four, is the dog today."

Arnie P. looked up at Dempsey quizzically.

"It's an expression," the man said. "Anyway, that gives us an average of eighty-two. Not great," he admitted, "but it's opening day."

"Not bad at all," echoed Vince. "At least it's an honest eighty-two."

Pearsall nodded. "I can live with that."

"I believe we owe a couple of those stokes to your little friend," Clawson stated, nodding towards the terrier.

"He's right, Travis," Pearsall agreed. "I thought it was a pretty stupid idea at first, but you pulled it off."

"I didn't pull anything off," protested Dempsey. "I just don't see as well as I used to, is all."

"None of us do," Verdu admitted. "But it was a pretty clever solution."

They were taking another look at the scorecard when McTavish wandered by.

"And how was the round today, gentlemen?"

"Not bad, Mac." Dempsey stepped up and showed the

man their card. "We'll get better with practice."

The stocky Scotsman looked the card over and did the calculations.

"Eighty-two? Not bad, but Muck and his boys scored a seventy-five today."

"Seventy-five?" Pearsall's eyes grew large in amazement.

"Shit!" Verdu muttered under his breath and turned away.

"Well, boys," Clawson smiled, "we need to improve our game a bit, it seems, or we're going to have to see that gawd awful suit again."

"And playing like this," Dempsey acknowledged, "ensures another sartorial insult from our club's fashion plate.

"The Victory Tux." Pearsall grumbled, shuddering involuntarily.

"You might be right," McTavish agreed, "but it's early yet."

He looked down and smiled at Arnie P.

"And how did Mr. P do today?"

"He followed the rules to the letter."

"That's good to know," McTavish said. "Was he a good nabbler?"

"Nabbler?"

"Did he help?"

Dempsey nodded. "On a number of occasions."

McTavish scratched his head through his tam. "And I suppose you've ruled out glasses, then?"

It was the question that had been on everyone's mind. Why not get glasses if you have trouble seeing the ball? It's what people do, after all.

Dempsey reddened. "Glasses don't help," he stated. "Besides, my vision's fine. It's just when the ball leaves the fairway, I...well..."

"Lose sight of it?"

"Exactly."

"So I thought," nodded McTavish, a wisp of a smile darting across his face. "So, we'll be seeing Mr. P. again, will we?"

The dog barked excitedly. The Scotsman reached down and gave the terrier a rough pat.

"It won't be a problem, will it?"

The weathered Scot in the green kilt cocked his head and fixed his dark gray eye on Dempsey.

"If you can see it coming, lad, it's not a problem."

The words hung in the air as the man walked away.

"I wonder what that was all about," Pearsall asked.

"There's no way of knowing," Clawson answered.

Verdu took the scorecard from Dempsey.

"Come on, guys. We gotta get this in before time expires."

Dempsey nodded, but he was watching McTavish as the short man walked away. What was the man trying to tell him? Was he trying to tell him anything?

He put the thoughts out of his mind and fell in behind the others as they headed off towards the scorer's office.

Arnie P. brought up the rear, a spring in his step as he took in all the new sights and smells around him.

* * * * *

Many wealthy people in the world use their money and stature to create charitable institutions. Those with less ambition just contribute to charitable institutions, though given the amount they contribute they could just as easily start their own. Others create trust funds, or sponsor events that aid the less fortunate. Still others endow schools, universities, hospitals, or museums with funds for scholarships and research. All told, the moneyed in America, by and large, are a kindly, charitable group who, either from a sense of caring, love, guilt, or largesse, use their resources to help the less fortunate of the world.

Tiberius Julian Muck, who had amassed more money than he could ever spend, was not part of that group. A self-made multi-millionaire, Muck had struggled long and hard for everything he had, starting life poor and relentlessly clawing his way upwards, and he was not about to throw it away on those he saw as unwilling to care for themselves. He was a hard man, both physically and figuratively, the natural outcome of seeing all things in life through the prism of competition.

He'd worked hard for thirty years to build a thriving, interstate construction empire, believing that his focus and diligence alone accounted for his success. He would never concede that luck played any part in his fortune. To do that would mean that there were elements of his life that he couldn't control. A man made his own luck, he would say, just as a man would take whatever steps were needed to succeed.

"Where are you going with Cali?"

Julia Muck, T.J.'s wife of twenty years, was a tall, slender brunette with a gentle nature, the patience of a saint, and a spine of steel when needed. Anyone who'd met the Mucks wondered what the two had seen in each other, especially what she'd seen in him. After getting to know T.J., those same people wondered why Julia would stay with him. Like most wives, she was not blind to her husband's failings. As long as those failings stayed outside of their lives, she was willing to tolerate what others thought of her husband.

"Out back," Muck declared.

Muck had a lob wedge in one hand, a bag of golf balls in the other, and was being followed closely by a jet black Doberman Pincer, its brown, torpedo-shaped snout tilted expectantly up at Muck.

Julia had many more questions to ask her husband, but she could tell by the set of his jaw and hooded eyes that now was not the time.

"Don't keep him long," Julia cautioned.

Muck led the Doberman into the spacious back yard, past the pool, and out a gate at the far end of the manicured property. Through the gate was a deep, broad, untended field, still his property.

Caligula, or Cali as he was known, had been the loyal family pet for seven years, the last in a long series of

Dobermans. He was a large, muscular specimen, as imposing in his own way as was his master in his.

Muck dumped the bag of balls at his feet, coaxing one of the balls out of the group with the head of his golf club.

He'd heard from a few of the other members about Dempsey's dog. Why the arrogant prick didn't just get glasses was beyond him, but the thought that the dog could help him spot balls was intriguing. Not that it would change the outcome of the tournament. As with most things in his life, Muck would do whatever was necessary to win, whether in business or golf.

He addressed the ball. His swing was slow and practiced. The ball sailed skyward, falling into the high weeds thirty yards away.

Cali, sitting six feet away, watched the ball vanish into the weeds, then looked back at Muck. He had no idea what was going on, but if his master enjoyed it and wanted him to watch, the Doberman would sit and watch.

Muck mumbled a curse under his breath. He set up another ball.

But it wasn't the glasses, was it? The thing about the glasses was just a ruse. It had to be. Dempsey was up to something. The dog wasn't there to help find balls. He was sure of that. No, the dog was there to help Dempsey and his asshole friends cheat. They wanted the trophy. Everyone wanted that trophy, but he was the only one that would have it.

Muck sent the next shot forty yards into the field. Cali watched expectantly.

Muck had come up with some very creative ways to play the game of golf, but he had to admit that Dempsey had hit upon a very subtle, very clever way to beat the system. If he didn't dislike the guy so much he might even respect the man's resourcefulness. Hell, Muck himself had devised some very creative ways to score his team's rounds, methods that had proven themselves over the years, and he wasn't above simply kicking a ball into a better lie. It was crude. It was artless. It was golf. It was how the game was played, regardless of what that scrawny

Scot had to say. And the fact that Dempsey might have found a better way to win, well, that just wouldn't stand.

"Well?" Muck stared hard at Cali, his tone taking on an unpleasant edge. "Go get the ball."

Cali recognized the tone. The Doberman blinked nervously and looked away, not sure what was expected of him.

Muck set up another ball.

He couldn't let Dempsey win.

The ball flew into the distant weeds.

"Go get it, Cali."

Dempsey was up to something, and he wasn't going to pull one over on ol' Muck.

"Go get the ball!"

The dog shifted nervously, a soft whimper escaping his throat. He looked out into the field. The Dobie stood and took a tentative step towards the green expanse. He looked back over his shoulder.

Muck dropped the club and pulled his belt from his pants. Doubling the leather strap, he struck it into the palm of his hand. The loud 'clap' was not a foreign sound to the dog, nor was the feeling of the strap along his flanks.

Muck took a step towards the dog.

He was not going to let Dempsey make a fool of him.

JULY

By the Fourth of July weekend, to no one's surprise, Muck, Baxter, Pfunke, and Howe were in first place, with a comfortable eight-stroke lead over the second place team. Dempsey, Pearsall, Verdu, and Clawson were in third place, twelve strokes back from the leader.

"Not an insurmountable lead," Pearsall stated, reviewing his copy of the standings. "And we're six up on number four."

It was early Saturday morning. The air was mild but heavy with the promise of humidity that, by midday, would be almost unbearable. The foursome hoped to be finished and in the bar by then.

Arnie P. sat obediently at Dempsey's feet, listening as the men talked. He'd come to recognize each man's voice and each man's tone. He decided that he liked them all, especially the tall one with the ebony skin.

"Who are those guys in second place?" Verdu studied the list.

Pearsall shrugged. "I don't recognize their names."

"I know Hendricks," acknowledged Dempsey. "He's the guy with a bad face lift and the gorgeous trophy wife."

Clawson shot his friend a disbelieving grimace.

"Travis," he stated, patiently, "this is Van Courtland Glen. There's more money concentrated in this one area of Fredericksburg than the rest of the region combined. Trophy wives and bad face lifts are as common as kudzu."

"Yeah," Verdu added. "You've just described half of the membership."

Dempsey nodded. "I think he's the ice cream guy..."

"...big facility up in Newington..."

"...and another in Lynchburg?"

"That's the one."

Clawson nodded, a pained look bolting across his face.

"What's with you," Dempsey asked, only mildly troubled by his Southern friend's expression.

"I just figured out who you were talking about."

"So?"

"It's nothing," Clawson said, dismissively.

"Get on with it, man." Pearsall playfully slapped Clawson's shoulder. "Tell us."

"There isn't anything to tell."

"There must be something," Verdu observed. "Maybe he just doesn't want to tell us."

"You think?" Pearsall taunted his brawny friend.

"Gentlemen," Clawson began, "though of little consequence now, I once dated Mrs. Hendricks..."

"The tall, curvaceous blond with the sculpted legs, firm breasts, and pouty lips?"

"I believe that accurately describes her."

"You dated her?" Pearsall rolled his eyes. "What's she like?"

"Intelligent, thoughtful, and well read, with a sparkling sense of humor."

"I meant..." Pearsall pressed.

"I know what you meant," chided Clawson.

"You dated a married woman?"

"Never," corrected a shocked Clawson. "I would never, ever knowingly jeopardize the sanctity of another's marriage." Clawson slowly folded the rating sheets and tucked them into his back pocket. "Suffice it to say that the lovely Mrs. Hendricks was not always a trophy wife."

"So, you knew her before she was married?"

"Repeatedly, I'd wager," Pearsall quipped, forcing a laugh from the others.

"Please," Clawson asked, "say what you will about me,

of my reprobate behavior, of my ill manners or lack of proper pedigree. It is nothing less than I deserve. But please do not demean Constance..."

"...Constance?"

"Mrs. Hendricks," he clarified. "She is a sweet, intelligent woman of fine, noble character, a woman that any man would be lucky to call his wife."

Dempsey, Pearsall, and Verdu stood speechless in the early morning sun. They had never, in their long friendship with Clawson, heard the man speak in such a manner. This brief glimpse into his world spoke volumes about the Southerner...and about the woman he felt duty bound to defend.

The other three men looked at each other, their eyes acknowledging what they each had tumbled to, just as their unspoken communication carried the mutual agreement to let the issue lie.

"I'm sorry," Pearsall said, offering Clawson his hand. "I meant nothing by my comments."

Clawson took the big man's hand.

"That's very kind of you, Mitch. Thank you."

The awkward silence that followed was quickly broken by the arrival of McTavish. Still dressed in his woolen kilt, jacket, and tam, it was a wonder the humidity hadn't turned him into a runny lump of trifle. Yet he wore the same outfit year round and seemed no worse for it.

"Back again, I see." McTavish nodded to each man in turn, a warm, sincere smile shared with the foursome. "You've got some competition."

"We noticed," stated Verdu. "It's one thing to have Muck in the lead, but to be bested by the Ice Cream King of the mid Atlantic?"

The wee Scot snorted. "Ice cream or no, he and his team are playing well. Granted, Hendricks is the weakest link in that chain, but the man is in his seventies. Many men his age have forgotten how to spell 'golf' much less play it."

"They are playing well," agreed Dempsey.

"Aye, they are that," confirmed McTavish, "but I think you can make up the strokes."

His voice lowered conspiratorially.

"They've started strong, but they've made the tyro's error of mistaking a distance match for a sprint. I don't think they can keep the pace they've set."

Pearsall's eyes narrowed in thought. "It's golf, Mac. One game a week is all they need."

McTavish winked. "Hendricks and his crew have decided they're takin' the cup. They've been playing four rounds a week. One for the books and three practice. It's a devilish pace. They may have the time and the desire, but they don't have the endurance."

Pearsall gave Dempsey a look, his eyebrows arched in a 'well-what-do-you-know' expression.

"So keep your pace, gentlemen. You don't have to do much more than keep the ball in play."

"Thanks, Mac." Verdu smiled.

The Scot nodded, then looked down at Arnie P. The Jack Russell had been sitting quietly, listening, his bright, expectant eyes turned upward.

McTavish squatted down next to the dog. He rubbed the dog's snout playfully.

"And you," he said, 'are going to have more company out there today."

"More?"

"Aye." McTavish stood. "It seems your idea has caught on. There'll be three more golf dogs out on the course this morning."

"Three?"

McTavish nodded. "And I'd put good money down that I'll be seeing more later today. The number will grow."

Dempsey mulled over the prospect of more dogs on the course. He'd seen a few dogs here and there, but had given them little thought. Still, he thought, the more dogs, the bigger the potential problem for McTavish.

"I'm really sorry about this," he said. "I had no idea..."

"Nor did I," McTavish interrupted. He raised a cautioning hand to stop Dempsey. "I had my suspicions, but you just never know about the weave until the fabric unfolds."

Clawson and Verdu exchanged a confused look.

"But there's no need to change anything. The same rules apply. The ball gets touched or moved and there's a penalty. The dog leaves 'treasures' on the course and the dog is banned from play."

"Still..."

McTavish waved Dempsey to silence.

"It's fine for now. Most folks aren't sure why they're bringing their dogs along anyway. They see you and your buddy here, they see your score, and they think there's some advantage to having a dog along. It won't last long for most, but it's better to let them try and fail than to bar the pups." He winked at Clawson and Verdu. "The best lessons are learned at the base of the stone, don't you agree?"

They nodded, more from reflex than from comprehension.

"Of course, that doesn't explain Muck."

"Muck?"

The Scotsman nodded. "The man brought his dog yesterday. Was a sad thing, really. The poor dog. Hasn't a clue what's expected of him. A fine looking Doberman. Not fond of the breed myself, mind you, but a fine looking dog all the same. But chasing small things isn't really in their nature," he opined, giving Arnie P. a nod. "Not like this one here. Muck had to chase the poor animal to the ball to get it to track."

"Defeats the purpose right there," Pearsall stated.

"Aye, but the rock-headed man was determined to get his dog to spot for him." He shook his head in disgust. "The way he beat the poor animal was criminal, it broke my heart. I tried to intervene, but to no avail. Still, they played their worst round ever yesterday, and if they're smart they'll leave the poor dog home and just go back to playing. It would be far less traumatic for Muck's partners and his dog."

"I hope you're right," Dempsey stated.

"But you know he won't," Clawson said.

"Why not?" Verdu looked wonderingly at the

Southerner.

"Because he's worried about us. He sees how we're playing, that Arnie P.'s out there tracking balls, is damned if we'll get some advantage that he doesn't have, and is just too obsessed with beating us to see that he's beating himself."

"I think you're right," agreed McTavish. "If it weren't for the whitecaps he wouldn't know there was a wind."

The four men standing around the Scot stared at one another, wondering if any of them understood what he meant.

"At any rate, I tell you this as a warning. Muck is not playing well and is taking it out on his dog. He may yet take it out on others," he said, shooting Arnie P. a concerned glance, "or their dogs. Keep an eye out."

McTavish wished them well and ambled off to speak with another foursome.

"That's a troubling thought," Pearsall admitted. "Muck out of control."

"He's not out of control," Clawson observed. "He's a sadistic megalomaniac who's so afraid of losing that he'd do anything to win."

The others nodded.

"So let's be careful," Dempsey said.

"And let's all keep an eye out for Arnie." Pearsall reached down and lifted the dog up to his face. He wouldn't admit it, but he'd grown quite fond of his partner's family pet.

Arnie P. returned the sentiment by excitedly licking Pearsall's face.

"That's right," Verdu smiled, chuckling. "After all, a dog in trouble is a chance to excel."

"Stop it," Dempsey laughed.

"You think they're real sayings from Scotland?" Pearsall looked from one of his friends to the other. He carried Arnie P. under one arm as he walked to the golf cart. "Or do you think he's just having us on?"

Clawson shrugged. "They sound authentic," he admitted, falling in step with the others. "They'd be more meaningful if I understood them, though."

"They'd be more meaningful," Verdu corrected, "if they meant something."

* * * * *

It became obvious after two holes that Verdu and Pearsall were playing team golf. Wherever Vince's ball went, Mitch's ball was sure to follow. On the opening drive, both men ended up in the trees. Their second shots were nearly identical hooks out of the trees, across the fairway, and into another stand of trees.

After bogeying the first hole, they started the second with wild drives into the left side rough. It wasn't shaping up to be one of their better rounds.

For Arnie P., things just didn't get any better.

To speed play, and to contain whatever bad golf *gris gris* the two men were sharing, Clawson switched carts with Pearsall at the third tee; since Vince and Mitch were putting their shots in the same spots, it seemed logical that they share a cart. And since their shots were more prone to loss than either Clawson's or Dempsey's, at least for this particular round, it was agreed that Arnie P. be dispatched as their designated spotter and cart mate.

"Take care of him, you two." Dempsey smiled as he watched his Jack Russell settle comfortably on the seat between the two men. "And behave yourselves. I don't want him picking up any bad habits."

Without looking back, Pearsall flipped his legal partner the bird.

"That's exactly what I'm talking about," Dempsey shouted after the cart.

Verdu, behind the wheel, accelerated away, steering towards the far side rough.

"It's going to be a long round," Clawson observed, double-checking to make certain his golf bag was secured to the cart.

Dempsey shrugged. "It's a nice day, and even with those two playing like they've never held a club before in their lives, we'll still beat the worst of the humidity and finish in plenty of time for the cookout."

The Fourth of July celebration at the club was a modest affair. Typically, a late afternoon barbeque of burgers and dogs, beer and potato salad, and some piped in martial music was the sum total of Van Courtland Glen's Independence Day celebration. The big club event, and the one the members most looked forward to, was the end-of-tournament Fall's Eve Gala, a formal, festive evening capped by a grand fireworks show.

Their drives sat in the middle of the fairway, within twenty feet of each other. Parking their cart next to their balls, Dempsey looked back to see Verdu, Pearsall, and Arnie P. searching the woods.

"They'll be a minute," he said.

Clawson nodded, looking off to his right. In the trees was another golfer searching for a shot. He was aided by a mature Golden Retriever. Nosing under some brush, the Retriever barked excitedly.

"Golf dogs." Clawson shook his head and smiled.

"What?"

"Isn't that what McTavish called them? Golf dogs?"

"I don't know," Dempsey responded. "The truth is I don't catch half of what that man says."

"FORE!"

Both men crouched in their seats as a ball slammed into the side of the cart. They turned to see Verdu at the edge of the trees.

"Sorry," he shouted.

Clawson waved as Dempsey backed the cart towards the other side of the fairway. The golf ball finding the side of their golf cart over a hundred yards away, given the wide-open space surrounding it, did not bode well for the round…or the health of the team.

That a sphere of 1.62 ounces in weight and 1.68 inches in diameter could consistently cause so much physical and emotional distress has been a constant source of mystery to golfers. At times, the small, white ball seemed to possess a malicious, contrarian, sometimes malevolent nature out of all proportion to its size, routinely going where it shouldn't, in apparent defiance of the laws of physics and aerodynamics. And it is only the novice player, or wholly uninitiated to the sport, that could stand out in the middle of a broad, open fairway, on a clear, windless day, with the nearest player over two hundred yards away, and believe completely and absolutely in the laws of probability that suggest the statistical impossibility of a person ever being hit by a golf ball.

"We should have worn helmets today," Clawson observed, watching carefully as Pearsall addressed his ball.

That Vince and Mitch were matching each other, stroke for stroke, was not lost on either man sitting in harm's way.

Luckily, Pearsall's shot went straight and true into the fairway.

"Well," Dempsey sighed, "that's a relief."

"Yeah," agreed Clawson. "We may yet survive the round."

They moved forward to their golf balls. As they stepped from the cart, Pearsall, Verdu, and Arnie P. zipped by.

Clawson pointed. "Over in the rough."

Pearsall waved and steered the cart in the direction indicated.

Clawson watched the cart as it made its way across the fairway. Dempsey thought that his friend was watching to make sure they found Verdu's ball, but it soon became clear that, while Clawson's eyes were on his golf partners, his mind was elsewhere.

"You know Mitch meant nothing by his comment, don't you?"

Rex, pulled from his contemplation, turned and nodded. "Of course he didn't. There's not one of you with a malicious bone in your bodies." He took a club from his bag. "And we've been together long enough to have earned the right of brotherly ball-busting."

He addressed his ball.

"I took no insult at what Mitch said. He's like a brother, granted a tall, black brother that my great, great ancestors might have cast a disapproving eye on, but a brother none the less, as are you and Vince, so your license to speak to me plainly, personally, is total."

He took a smooth, easy swing.

Dempsey watched as the ball landed a few feet in front of the green, and then rolled onto the firm putting surface.

"Nicely done."

"Thank you."

Dempsey selected a club and approached his ball.

"No," Clawson continued, "I took no offense."

The other man nodded. He settled into his stance.

"I'm just not over her yet."

Travis' eyes peeked up from under the brim of his ball cap.

"Sorry?"

"I'm in love with Constance Hendricks."

Dempsey's shot drifted a bit to the right but did manage to catch the edge of the green.

"Well, you wouldn't be the first man to fall in love with a married woman, Rex."

The Southerner nodded. "Except that she wanted to marry me."

"Come again?"

Clawson put his club in his bag and climbed into the cart. Dempsey was close behind.

"I met Constance about five years ago. Her maiden name was Kilgore, of the Savannah Kilgores. We started dating, but neither of us were that serious, or so I had thought."

"Rex, you're a confirmed bachelor."

"I'm a bachelor because I'm unmarried," he clarified, "and my confirmation was bestowed by married men with poor memories and rich fantasies."

Travis smiled sheepishly. He'd been one of those who'd just assumed that a wealthy, attractive young man would be content with playing the field. It had never occurred to him that his was not the only perspective on the topic, or that being married and having a family might be someone else's idea of the perfect life.

"So you want to get married?"

Clawson shrugged. "I neither seek it nor avoid it. For me, it's an option that life presents us and we either take it or we don't. I would not marry the wrong woman simply to be married," he stated, watching as Verdu's shot made it into the fairway and rolled towards the green. "On the other hand," he continued, turning to face Dempsey, "I may not have married the right woman simply to avoid the institution."

"I never imagined," Dempsey stated. He put the cart in gear and drove towards the green.

"Nor should you. I mean no disrespect to you or the others, but my private life is just that. Our dating, such as it was, was our business. To avoid the gossip and inevitable meddling, we were as circumspect as possible."

"Well, it worked," said Dempsey. "I never tumbled to it."

Clawson shrugged. "It seemed the thing to do at the time. Looking back on it, we did almost everything we possibly could to ensure that our relationship failed."

"Sounds like you were successful."

"Unfortunately, yes."

"And you didn't see it coming?"

"We were so intent on keeping others out of our lives that we really only managed to fully exclude each other."

Dempsey nodded.

"But not before we fell in love."

Pearsall and Verdu drove up to Vince's ball. The short, stocky man stepped from the cart, extracted a club from his bag, and made his shot onto the green.

Dempsey brought his cart to a stop near the green.

"Love is a strange, beautiful mix of motion, passion, thought, and uncertainty, and the mix is unique to each participant." Clawson made no move to leave the cart. "Our mix was perfect, but the timing was bad."

"I'm sorry to hear that."

"What can you do?" He exited the cart. "Most of human experience can be traced directly to missed opportunities."

"Still..."

"She's married." He smiled. "Happily so, I hope. For her

sake. Because it is what she wanted."

"Hendricks?"

"That's a question I've struggled with," Clawson admitted. He took his putter and stepped towards the green. "Constance is not a stupid woman, so I'm certain she had good reasons."

Dempsey followed Clawson towards the green.

People married for as many different reasons as there are people, Dempsey thought. It wouldn't be the first time he'd heard of a woman loving one man and marrying another, though he was never quite certain how that could succeed.

"Maybe she likes ice cream?"

Clawson laughed. "Maybe she does, Travis, but I doubt she'd marry the man for the discount."

At the edge of the green, Clawson stopped. He looked back to see Pearsall, Verdu, and Arnie P. pull up behind their cart.

"I trust you three with everything. Even with this, so if you choose to share it with Mitch and Vince, fine. But it can't go any further. She's a married woman and I'm a man with a rogue's reputation, underserved though it may be. We haven't spoken to one another since her marriage. I would not want our history to have any impact on her reputation or happiness."

"And your happiness?"

"I'll find it," he said, reassuring his friend, "just not with her, but that should have nothing to do with her life."

Dempsey thought it over, then nodded.

"I won't say a word to the others," he said. "It's your story to tell."

"Fair enough."

They stepped onto the green.

* * * * *

If football is a game of inches, golf is a game of millimeters.

As the round continued, Pearsall, and particularly

Verdu, managed to get their games under control. With a slight grip change, and an infinitesimal stance adjustment, the two men's shots stayed in play, helping to bring the team's score out of the stratosphere and into contention.

As the games improved, Arnie P.'s services were needed less and less. He seemed content to sit in the cart and watch the game, his ears perking slightly with the crack of the ball taking flight. He watched each shot expectantly, but the balls stayed true and in the fairway. For Arnie P., this particular round of golf became a pleasant morning drive through the countryside. This was fine with the bipeds, too, for while McTavish had mentioned only three other golf dogs out on this particular day, the team had already spotted twice that many dogs traveling with other foursomes. And other than a snow white Pekingese that Verdu thought he'd heard called 'Chop Suey', and was of a size and demeanor that all were certain would cause Arnie P. no problems, the other dogs on the course were large, varied in breed and, by all appearances, fairly aggressive.

On the seventh fairway, a charcoal Great Dane bitch emerged from the woods to the right of the team. Their drives had been grouped nicely in the center of the fairway so, along with Arnie P.'s warning, they'd had plenty of time to adjust to the other dog's approach. The dog appeared curious about the men, but intent on the golf balls. Neither fast nor slow, the Great Dane advanced on the foursome in a loping, almost comical fashion. As she neared Clawson, whose ball was nearest the dog, another golfer appeared from the woods behind the dog.

"Babe!" The woman's voice was an odd mixture of command and concern. "Babe, get over here."

The dog stopped and considered her owner over her shoulder.

"Yeah, Babe," encouraged Clawson, "go to mama."

None of the men moved as the dog's owner stormed from the woods.

"Dammit, Babe," she cursed, closing with the dog. "These balls belong to these guys. My ball is back in the woods."

"Babe doesn't seem like much of a baller," Pearsall observed. He'd eased closer to Clawson and chocked down on his club, unsure if a five iron was the right club for a Great Dane.

"She's okay," the owner said. She'd reached the dog and grabbed her by the collar. She tugged roughly. "She just doesn't always distinguish between my ball and others."

"Maybe she shouldn't be out here until she can?" Verdu's comment wasn't intended to be unkind, but the intent was lost on the owner.

"Maybe not," she answered, her tone taking on a sharp edge, "but I didn't start this. If some jackass comes up with a scheme to beat the system, why shouldn't I have benefit of it?"

The woman pulled Babe back towards the woods until the dog decided that was where she wanted to go. Once focused, the huge dog bounded off in search of her owner's missing ball.

"That was close," stated Clawson. "I couldn't tell what she was going to do."

Pearsall patted the Southerner on the shoulder.

"Don't worry," he said. "I had your back."

"But she was in front of me."

Dempsey laughed. "Yeah, she was gonna take a ball with her. It was just a question of which one."

"You're probably right." Verdu smiled, then gave Dempsey a wink. "Well, come on, jackass. It's your shot."

* * * * *

With the exception of the appearance of a number of additional dogs, seemingly from nowhere, the team's round concluded without further incident. Whatever golf virus had infected Mitch and Vince worked itself out by the time they got to the tenth hole.

"Not great," Clawson admitted, reviewing the score card, "but given where we started, we recovered nicely."

On their way to the pro shop, an agitated man

appeared from the around the corner of the clubhouse.

"Excuse me," he said, stopping the other men. "Have you seen a dog?"

The four men looked down at Arnie P. The Jack Russell cocked his head, waiting for someone to say something.

"Not that dog," the man quickly clarified.

Pearsall thought he recognized the man.

"It's Norton, isn't it?"

The other man nodded. "Andy Norton. And you're Pearson?"

"Pearsall. Mitch Pearsall."

They shook hands.

"How'd you hit 'em today?"

"Average," Norton confessed, "but after Puff Mommy ran off..."

"Puff Mommy?" Verdu wasn't certain he'd heard correctly. "What's a Puff Mommy?"

"My wife's Samoyed. Good sized, cream-colored bitch. Sweet girl but can't always find the food bowl without help, if you know what I mean."

Dempsey nodded.

"But Puff Mommy?"

Norton shrugged. "My wife's idea. What can I tell you? Anyway, she ran off around the 15th on the North. Thought she might have made her way back here."

"We've seen a number of dogs today," Pearsall confirmed, "but we haven't seen yours."

"She'll kill me," Norton mumbled. "She loves that dog."

"She'll show up, Andy." Clawson tried to be encouraging. "We'll keep an eye out."

"I'd appreciate it," he said. "My wife got the dog to keep her company while I played golf. Losing the dog while playing golf will just be too much for her."

"Why even bring the dog?"

Norton's expression changed from anxious to wistful.

"So I can win the trophy."

"A dog can't help you do that," Dempsey said.

"Not now."

Norton's face brightened. "I need a better dog. A smarter dog." Norton's eyes grew distant. "A dog that can find lost balls, and help with club selection."

"Club selection?" Verdu looked from one of his friends to the next, hoping he'd misunderstood.

Norton returned from his mental side trip.

"Well, maybe not club selection, but certainly a better baller."

"Of course," Pearsall agreed, keeping his tone neutral. "Anyway, we'll keep an eye out for Puff Mommy."

Norton nodded and hurried off to query a foursome just finishing their round.

"What have you done, Travis?"

"Me?"

"You've opened a can of worms," Clawson observed, "or should I say a kennel of dogs, the likes of which has never been seen before."

"I wasn't trying to game the rules," Dempsey insisted, though even he thought his argument lacked some weight. The idea had come about by his need to see what he was doing, but had been driven by a desire to win, to beat Muck. He hadn't consciously plotted the use of Arnie P. as a way to exploit the rules of the game. On the other hand, he was a skilled, highly educated attorney. His mind approached the world from the perspective of finding ways through the law. Had he unconsciously planned this ruse? Was it possible?

"Whatever you were planning," Pearsall said," didn't work out the way you imagined." He looked hard at his law partner. "At least, I'd like to think you didn't plan for this to happen."

Dempsey looked down at Arnie P. Had he planned to exploit the family pet? He didn't think so, but was he that far removed from Norton's worldview?

Arnie P. gave his master an encouraging 'yip'.

Travis Dempsey looked at his golf partners.

"Honestly, I don't know what I thought would happen. At the time, being able to find a lost ball seemed like a good thing. I still think it's a good thing. But maybe I was wrong to involve Arnie P."

Clawson started laughing.

"Listen to you." He bent over and patted the dog on the head. "You're trying to improve your golf game, not build a master race of canines on the dried and broken bones of humanity."

He stood and resumed walking towards the clubhouse.

"Maybe it wasn't the brightest idea you've ever had," Clawson continued, "but as ideas go you get max points for originality. And you've proven a very important, valuable point, whether you've stopped to think about it or not."

"What's that," Verdu asked.

"This grand scheme of his hasn't worked."

Pearsall nodded. "There is that."

"We're well into the competition, Arnie P. has been with us from the very beginning, and we're in third place." He turned his head towards the dog. "No reflection on you, of course."

Arnie P., walking at Dempsey's heel, barked his understanding.

"So, if you've concocted some grand, devious master plan to subvert the rules of golf to our advantage, now's the time to throw the switch." Clawson stopped and faced Dempsey. "On the other hand, if, as I suspect, you hit upon an idea that you thought might give us an edge against Muck, well, it failed. I'm sure it's not the first idea you've had that didn't work..."

"...thanks..."

"...but remember, we all went along with it. Hell, it sounded good to me. It still sounds good. The problem isn't that we're losing a lot of balls, it's that we're just not playing as well as we'd like."

"Yeah," Vince offered, "if we were playing better we wouldn't need Arnie P."

"I don't know," Pearsall stated. "I like having the little guy around."

The tall man reached down and picked up the terrier. Arnie P. nibbled playfully at the man's earlobe.

"What about the other dogs?"

"What about 'em," Clawson countered. "McTavish made that call, and the dog owners make their decision about bringing their pets to the course. You may have opened the door, Travis, but you weren't forcing folks through it."

Travis nodded. All he'd wanted was a chance to win. They all had, and they all still did, but their winning would have everything to do with their level of play, and nothing to do with Arnie P.

"I mean, what's the worst that's going to happen?" Clawson stopped at the door to the clubhouse. "A bunch of folks bring their dogs out to the course, some go missing for a few days, a dog or two shits on a green, and Muck wins the Van Courtland Cup."

"Again."

Clawson smiled. "Gentlemen, let's not lose sight of the fact that golf, for all of its traditions, myths, and wonder, is still just a game. When all is said and done, win, lose, or draw, my penis is just as big as it's always been."

Dempsey sighed. "Thanks, Rex. I couldn't have said it any better myself."

"Except, maybe," Verdu offered, "for the penis thing."

"Yes," Dempsey agreed quickly, "except for the penis thing."

* * * * *

The old, red brick Sentinel Building had been a fixture on the corner of Sunken Road and Monroe Street since the turn of the century. Originally built as the home office of the long defunct Fredericksburg Sentinel...a local paper whose lofty goals had far outreached its revenues...the three story building had remained vacant for almost twenty years before enterprise, and the 70s, had changed its fate.

Situated across the street from the campus of the University of Mary Washington, the location was perfect for a cluster of small shops and cafés, a sort of urban mini-mall that catered to college students. Over the years the types of businesses had changed... record stores supplanting the head shops, and the small cafés morphing into coffee shops and burger joints...but the basic plan had taken root and prospered.

By the 90s, some of the shops were taken over by charitable organizations, most of which appealed to the young, idealistic nature of the nearby college population. The environmentalists were represented, as were the Tibetan Freedom Fighters. One group was the United Fellowship for the Liberation of Animals Confined and Detained and Controlled, or UFLACADAC. A serious, passionate group of young people who believed strongly in the rights of animals to be free, the Uffies, as they were known, were active on campuses across the country and throughout the world.

The UFLACADAC office, on the second floor of the Sentinel Building, was a local outreach facility, as well as the regional information center. Almost all of the workers were volunteers, with the vast majority of them from the university. It was a cheap, dedicated labor pool whose idealism, energy, and naivety worked for the benefit of the organization.

"That's right, ma'am. If whales had arms they'd be heart surgeons."

Miranda, an attractive, petite college sophomore spoke earnestly into the phone.

"So whaling isn't much different than going over to the local hospital, rounding up all the surgeons, and driving stakes through their hearts."

The young woman listened intently to the person on the other end of the phone, her big, brown eyes focused on a framed picture of a breaching whale. A small banner reading "Please don't kill me" was superimposed along the bottom of the photo.

"Of course we wouldn't kill surgeons," Miranda assured the caller, "so why would we kill whales?"

She listened.

"That's correct. Whaling is no longer legal, but whales are still dying. They need our help."

Miranda looked up and smiled at the young man sitting

at a desk across the narrow office.

Josh was a rising senior at Mary Washington. Tall and slender, with oily, shoulder length hair and thick glasses, Josh was not much to look at. A passionate, committed activist, he limited himself in what he'd wear, what he'd eat, and in the personal hygiene products he'd use...there was one natural deodorant soap that he used that left him smelling vaguely of a newly paved road. His was a life that had 'lonely' written all over it.

He returned Miranda's smile, allowing his mind to jump briefly from saving animals to picturing his fellow Uffie laying naked next to him in bed. He'd been taken with Miranda since she'd joined UFLACADAC...he'd been her trainer and mentor...and there was just something about her slender body, topped with dust colored hair, that distracted him in ways UFLACADAC detractors never did. She was out of his league, a sad realization for any male at the door to manhood, but maturity carried its own burdens, he often reminded himself, and one such burden was in knowing when a cause was lost.

"Well, ma'am, we have a program where you can adopt a whale...no, ma'am, they don't come live with you. You sponsor a whale through your contribution...yes, you can give the whale a name if you'd like...Zerubbabel is an odd name for a whale, but if that's your choice...yes, ma'am. We'll send you a picture of your whale, suitable for framing...uh huh...the cost is one hundred dollars."

She rolled her eyes. Discussions of money were always awkward, but Miranda had gotten used to it. After all, her awkwardness in soliciting contributions was far less painful than a harpoon in the back.

"I know it sounds like a lot of money, but you get the picture of your whale, you get to name your whale, and we send you a map showing you where Zerubbabel will be each month of the year...that's right, a map. You can show your friends at the nursing home...I'm sorry...of course, you're right...your friends at the mature adult living facility...where Zerubbabel is and what he looks like. In fact, your friends might like to adopt their own whales. If there are enough of you, we can put you all together in your own pod..."

Josh gave her a strained look.

Miranda shrugged. "...it's what they call a group of whales, ma'am...that's right...so, can I put you down for one hundred?"

She nodded and gave Josh the thumbs up.

As Miranda took the information from the contributor, Josh went over to a row of battered, mismatched filing cabinets. Opening one folder, he extracted a glossy photo of a whale breaching. The photo was identical to the one on Miranda's desk, though larger. There were eight such folders in the drawer, each full of a different shot of a whale doing cute, endearing, whaley things.

In another folder, in another drawer, he extracted a copy of a folded world map. The map had various colored lines and arrows snaking their way through the oceans, each depicting the migratory paths of whales around the world. He took the photo and map over to the office's only computer station.

"Thank you, ma'am. We'll get that right out to you."

Miranda hung up the phone.

"How do you spell..." Josh began, then realized he couldn't remember how to pronounce the name. "What was it?"

"Zerubbabel," she stated.

"Zerubbabel?" He waited, his fingers poised over the keyboard.

She consulted the contribution form in front of her. "Z-E-R-U-B-B-A-B-E-L."

"Oh," he said, "just like it sounds."

"I guess." Miranda jotted some notes onto the form.

Josh busied himself preparing the package for mailing. Working from a computerized template, he typed in the name of the whale. Miranda brought him the contribution form and he typed in the contributor's name and address.

Once everything was set, he fed the picture into the printer and hit the 'enter' key. On the back of the photo was printed the detailed information on Zerubabble, The Whale.

It was standard whale information, not at all unique to Zerubabble, but few contributors seemed to notice, or care.

"What is it today?"

Miranda and Josh looked up to see Taffy enter the cramped office.

Taffy was also a sophomore at the university, but where Miranda was perky and groomed, Taffy went more for the subdued, Earth Mother look. Her wardrobe consisted of flip-flops, recycled paper peasant dresses, university sweatshirts, and red cowboy bandanas. A true child of the Universe, she was a vegan who eschewed shaving, deodorants, scented soaps or perfumes, and any product that might have the remotest association with the timber or oil industries, automotives, cosmetics, Wall Street, or the military industrial complex. As a consumer, her strong beliefs severely limited her buying options. As a functioning member of society, her grooming choices limited how close people were willing to get to her.

"Whales," Josh answered. He watched Taffy closely to see which way she went around the desks. He needed to go in the opposite direction. She was a nice enough person, but if you didn't catch her within an hour after bathing, especially during the summer months, she ripened quickly and her aroma was overpowering.

Taffy nodded, tossing her backpack onto a nearby desk, slumping into a chair. She sighed loudly.

Both Miranda and Josh recognized the symptoms of Taffy's building emotional state. They'd learned the hard way that ignoring her moods only made them worse, and the worse they got, the more needy Taffy became. And the more needy Taffy became, the more she craved human contact, which meant that she would move closer to her coworkers and friends.

Josh gave Miranda a pleading look, but the younger Uffie shook her head.

"So, Taffy," he started, shooting Miranda a withering glance, "what's on your mind?"

"Nothing," she answered, staring intently at the ratty edges of one of her nails, "except that I hate my family."

Taffy's hatred of her family was neither new nor surprising. Her feelings about her parents, siblings, aunts, and uncles, all living in Fredericksburg and all extremely well off, were common knowledge among the other Uffies. Whether real or imagined, Taffy's family was always doing something to personally embarrass her, or irrevocably alter the natural order of the Universe. A passionate idealist, Taffy was unforgiving of anyone who didn't share her beliefs or worldview. In Taffy's world, refusing to recycle a plastic bag was tantamount to infanticide. Driving anything other than a Prius was the moral equivalent of opening an extermination camp. But the most objectionable offense her family had committed, the offense for which they were unlikely to ever find redemption, was that they were wealthy Conservatives who loved their daughter, gladly paying for her education, and patiently tolerating her scathing vitriol about their beliefs, actions, and life style. Taffy never seemed to tumble to the notion that her family's patience and forbearance allowed her to be the passionate extremist she had become, and that without their support she might have to get a real job, not to mention using deodorant.

Josh and Miranda shared an understanding look. They'd been down this road with the young woman before. The best course of action was to settle in for the ride.

"What have they done this time," asked Miranda.

The young woman shook her head in disgust.

"It's my uncle."

"Your uncle?"

"Yeah. He's an avid golfer. A member of Van Courtland."

The golf club was so well known that even those with little interest in the sport knew of it.

"I'm impressed," Josh declared.

"Well," Taffy snapped, "don't be. He's the worst type of animal abuser there is."

"What do you mean?" Miranda's interest was growing.

"What does it sound like I mean?"

Miranda gave the other woman a patient smile.

"I was over at my folk's house last night. A big dinner. Uncle John was telling me about what's happening at the club."

She looked to her fellow Uffie's, her eyes growing moist.

"They're using family pets as tracking animals," she moaned. "It's bad enough that my uncle has pets, or my parents, for that matter, but to force poor Fritz Bones Frizzles into slavery, well..."

"Fritz what?"

"Fritz Bones Frizzles. The cutest Australian terrier you'll ever want to meet." She sobbed. "And now he's gone."

Miranda, sensing that the other woman could use a hug, moved towards Taffy to offer comfort. The closer she got, the more pungent her associate became. She stopped a few feet away and settled into a nearby chair.

"I'm so sorry," Miranda said. "Did it happen quickly?"

Taffy nodded. "One minute he was there, the next he was gone."

"He's probably in a better place," opined Josh, philosophically.

Taffy stopped and looked hard at her fellow Uffie.

"What are you talking about?"

"Fritz Bones Frizzles," he answered. "He's dead, right?"

"I didn't say dead," she corrected. "I said 'gone.'"

"You mean..."

"...gone. The dog is gone."

Miranda shrugged, hoping for clarification.

"They're using dogs, family pets, to track golf balls at their club tournament. It seems to be all the rage. Some sort of twisted status thing. People bring their family pets to the course and the dogs are forced to run around that big, open golf course and chase after golf balls all day long."

Miranda wasn't sure she understood clearly what Taffy was saying. Josh understood, he just wasn't clear on where the problem lay.

"So the dogs are getting out more? Clean air? Exercise?"

"Exactly, Josh." Her tone was chilling. "Sorta like slaves

in the cotton fields."

The man reddened.

Miranda stepped in quickly. "So, what's your point?"

"The point," Taffy began, "is that animals are being exploited by humans, again. Conditions are so bad, so detestable and demeaning, that many of the poor animals have run off."

"Run off?"

"Yes, run off. To escape their shackles."

Josh wondered if they'd run off because of the abuse, which didn't sound much like abuse at all, or because the dogs had a chance to run off? He'd grown up with dogs. No matter how loyal a dog was, they liked to run away. They generally came back tired, hungry, dirty, and chagrinned, but they did come back.

He considered sharing his experience with Taffy, but discarded the idea. She had her mind made up. Best to let her go. She'd get it out of her system and then they could all move on.

"How many dogs have run away?"

Unobserved by the others, a tall, slender man had entered the office. Dressed completely in black, his pale complexion seemed to glow, which lent a certain radiance to his glacial blue eyes. His long, black hair was pulled into a tight ponytail, making his face look even narrower than it was.

He was a striking man. Seeing him for the first time, it would be hard assigning him an age, though he was in his late forties. Passing him on the street a person might think him to be an artist or musician, someone on the creative fringe, poised to catapult into the mainstream spotlight. It was an aura he cultivated. It opened many doors for him that might otherwise remain closed.

He was Leigh Wolfe, head of the regional UFLACADAC office, and one of the organization's founders.

"Oh, Leigh." Taffy was up and into his arms instantly. Both Miranda and Josh winced, imagining what Wolfe was smelling, though the older man appeared not to notice.

"Calm yourself, Taffy." He led her back to her chair. "Tell me everything, from the beginning."

Taffy recounted all she knew about the tournament, the dogs, her uncle, and the whole sorry mess. Wolfe listened quietly, his face betraying no emotion. When the young woman was finished, he nodded.

"So mankind has devised yet another means of abusing our friends in the animal kingdom."

Josh cleared his throat. "Leigh, I'm not so certain that there's a problem here."

"You may be right, Josh. We'll check it out, but according to Taffy, there are close to fifteen dogs loose in the wilds of Spotsylvania County, all due to the thoughtless exploitation of some rich, fat cat sportsmen..."

"...and women," added Miranda.

"...and women," Leigh agreed. "The point is, it is just this sort of wrong that UFLACADAC was founded to correct. We speak for those who do not speak our language. We represent those who cannot hold a pen and write to their congressmen..."

"...and women," Miranda hastened to add again.

"...and women. Yes, Miranda, thank you. We help those who do not understand our world. And we embrace those who crave freedom, universal peace, and interspecies understanding as passionately and as tirelessly as we do."

He was a passionate man, one who believed strongly in his mission.

"We must do all we can to help these...what did your uncle call them, Taffy?"

"Golf dogs."

Wolfe nodded. "We must help these golf dogs to throw off their shackles and live free."

It was a noble cause, he knew. It was just the sort of cause UFLACADAC had been organized to champion, but they had lost their way. They needed to be refocused.

He looked at the expectant faces before him.

"Here's what I want each of you to do."

AUGUST

The news of Hendricks' death caught everyone by surprise, and reactions to the news were as varied as the speculation concerning the cause. There was a brief, two-paragraph article in the Fredericksburg Journal explaining, in the vaguest of terms, the passing of the Ice Cream King of Virginia.

Since most had never heard of the man, his passing went mostly unnoticed. At the Van Courtland Glen Country Club, the news couldn't have been bigger.

It was the fourth of August, a Saturday, and a notification on the tournament announcement board in the pro shop had stated only that there was an emergency meeting for all tournament participants in the banquet hall. Understanding that not everyone would see the note, e-mails had been sent out the night before, along with late evening phone calls. Every effort was made to round up all players. Almost all were in attendance. Those who didn't get the word, well, they would know soon enough.

"Thank you for being here this morning." McTavish, at the front of the room, looked around at all the expectant faces. "A special thanks to those of you who came in especially for this meeting."

The Scotsman cleared his throat.

"Now," continued McTavish, "we have a change in the standings."

The murmurs filling the room sounded like a hive of honeybees whose home had just been swatted with a stick.

McTavish waved the room to silence.

"Some of you may have heard that Mr. Hendricks passed away last night."

Clawson, sitting with the others, looked to his friends, confused. "What did he say?"

"The details of his passing are sketchy," the Scot continued, "and even were I to know them, this would not be the place to discuss them. But it is important because, according to the tournament rules, a team cannot continue without all of its original members."

The room became as quiet as a tomb.

"My sincere apologies to the surviving members of the team," McTavish said, "but the rules must be adhered to, or the Clyde will spill its banks."

The Scot took in the blank faces staring back at him.

"Right, then," he said. "The disqualification moves Mr. Dempsey's team into second place, and the rest move up a slot as well. So, seven strokes now separate the number one and number two teams."

Dempsey, Verdu, Pearsall, and Clawson exchanged disbelieving looks. Their fortunes had changed instantly.

Clawson was the first to recover.

"I'll meet you at the first tee," he said, rising from his chair.

"Where's he going," Pearsall asked.

"To make a call would be my guess," answered Verdu. He watched the lean Southerner exit the room by a side door.

"We need him focused," Pearsall said.

"He's focused," confirmed Dempsey, "just not on the game."

Pearsall nodded absently.

"That's all I had," the Scot declared. "Good luck if you're playing today, and thanks to the rest of you for coming out so early."

"Hell of a way to move up in the standings," Pearsall observed, absently receiving the congratulations of departing golfers.

"Hell of a way to accomplish anything," added Verdu, "but we didn't kill the man."

"I wonder what happened," asked Dempsey.

"Who knows," Verdu answered. "Maybe Rex will find out."

"Maybe so."

Pearsall checked his watch. "Don't we have an 8:40 tee time?"

* * * * *

"Five more minutes, Mr. Dempsey," declared the starter, "and then you'll be penalized."

Dempsey nodded at the gray haired man sitting in the booth next to the first tee. Under normal circumstances, getting out of the box late wouldn't have been an issue, but because they'd declared the round, a 'prompt start' rule applied. If they didn't start their drives within ten minutes of their scheduled tee time, they would each be assessed a penalty stroke on their best hole of the round, a daunting consideration when pars could make the difference between picking up a few strokes on the leader, or falling far back into the pack.

Dempsey looked to Pearsall and Verdu. The tall black man, standing next to the cart and petting Arnie P's head, shrugged, something he did with great effect in the courtroom, usually to underscore a logical paradox or factual impossibility put forth by opposing counsel's witnesses. Today's shrug, however, was an honest manifestation of uncertainty.

Verdu stood on the tee, his ball resting on its white pedestal. The muscular man rocked from side to side, staying as loose as possible. At the last possible moment, he would begin the round with his drive.

Arnie P. looked up and barked excitedly.

"Here he comes," Pearsall roared.

From the far side of the clubhouse Clawson trotted down the brick path.

The starter checked his watch. Dempsey signaled Verdu. The man took a practice swing, then settled into his stance and drove his ball two hundred and seventy yards down the center of the fairway.

"Well," he said, retrieving his tee and stepping from the tee box, "at least we're off to a good start."

"One minute until the next drive," the starter declared. He looked from his watch to Dempsey.

"You need to be less consumed with time." Dempsey smiled at the man. With driver in hand, he entered the tee box.

Clawson made it to the cart and pulled his driver from his bag.

Dempsey's drive ended on the right side of the fairway, ten yards shorter than Verdu's.

"Sorry for the delay, gentlemen." Clawson, slightly winded, took a second to catch his breath.

Pearsall patted the Southerner on the shoulder. "You made it, Rex. That's what matters."

The third drive, Pearsall's, sailed too high to be a long drive, and too short to be a good drive, but it was straight.

"A little under that one," he admitted.

"Still got close to two hundred," Dempsey observed. "Makes for a long par four, but doable."

Clawson stepped to the tee. He took a deep, cleansing breath, focused on the ball, and sent his drive off to the right. The Jack Russell watched the ball closely, anxious to play. Before anyone could think of the disaster an errant drive might cause, the ball began drawing back towards the edge of the fairway. The ball hit the ground just inside the edge of the tightly cut grass and took off down the fairway, angling towards the center.

The ball rolled to a stop three hundred yards away.

"Christ, Rex," muttered Verdu. "Can you do that again?"

"Let's hope so," he answered. His smile broadened slowly, beginning with his lips and inching outward towards his ears.

"Yeah," Pearsall agreed. "Let's hope so."

"Maybe we should have him trot from green to tee," Dempsey suggested. "A little aerobic workout before the drive seems to work wonders."

Clawson just smiled.

As they made their way to the carts, no one was sure what to say.

Dempsey and Clawson climbed into their cart and drove off.

"I assume you're not smiling just because of the drive?"

Clawson shook his head.

"Life is a funny thing," he said, his southern accent a bit thicker than usual.

"It is," Dempsey agreed, steering the cart down the fairway. "Still, people don't just wander around with shit-eating grins on their faces because life is a funny thing."

"True enough," Clawson agreed, "and you should know that Hendricks' death is a tragic occurrence."

"But...?"

"It does open doors."

"I got that point." Dempsey stopped the cart beside his ball. "Is your friend okay?"

"Under the circumstances."

"And those are...?"

Clawson shook his head and chuckled. "That's what makes life such a funny thing."

"Go on," urged Dempsey.

"Hendricks died of a massive coronary."

"That's funny?"

"Not at all."

Dempsey nodded, his eyes growing thoughtful, distant.

"That's how I want to go," he said. "Peacefully, in my sleep."

Clawson looked wonderingly at his friend. "He didn't go in his sleep," he said, "and I don't get the impression it was too peaceful, either."

"Oh?" Dempsey stepped from the cart and considered his next shot. He pulled a club from his bag. Only then did Clawson's words filter through to his conscious mind.

"What do you mean he didn't go peacefully?"

"Well, I'm not certain that I have the whole story, or that all my facts and details are accurate, but it seems that our Mr. Hendricks, the Ice Cream King, had a private life that, unlike his products, was not intended for public consumption."

Dempsey's eyes narrowed. "What? He buggered little boys?"

Clawson shook his head. "Nothing that 'out there'," he said, then thought better of his answer. "Well, maybe it was 'out there', but it was all consensual."

Dempsey's confusion was growing. Still, he nodded weakly, addressed the ball, and took a measured swing. The ball landed just short of the green.

"Nice shot," Clawson said.

"Don't change the subject," Dempsey responded. "Give."

They drove over to Clawson's ball.

"Hendricks was into kink," Clawson started. "Leather, whips, water, you name it, you imagine it, he'd already done it."

"Hendricks?" Dempsey had a hard time imagining the small, portly, balding man with the florid complexion as a closet deSade, much less being able to attract the necessary playmates. Still, it probably had less to do with his drives and interests than with his ability to fund his intimate playtimes. Money is the great "enhancer," he thought; it makes the ugly attractive, the feeble attractive, the lame attractive, the stupid attractive, and the attractive even more so. A sad commentary, perhaps, but it explained a lot in life.

"Go figure," Clawson agreed, sharing much the same thought as Dempsey. "Apparently, he was in bed with two Asian women who, having hand cuffed him to the bed, blindfolded him, and inserted a vibrator into a spot I can't imagine putting anything that moves, took turns riding him like a race horse, crops and all."

Dempsey stood there, eyes wide in disbelief. "A vibrator?"

Clawson shrugged. "Seems his heart gave out."

"Well, there's a surprise," Dempsey commented, not trying to mask his sarcasm.

He brought the cart to a stop near Clawson's ball.

"To each his own," the Southerner offered. He stepped from the cart and grabbed a club.

"His wife must have been shocked when she found the body." Dempsey tried to imagine what that would be like. The shame. The embarrassment. The anger.

"Oh, he had the good sense to take his hobbies elsewhere."

His shot landed within five feet of the flag.

"Constance didn't find the body," Clawson continued. "She was notified, and she had to identify the body, but old man Hendricks never took that hobby home."

"I guess that's good news," Dempsey said. "For Constance."

Clawson chuckled. "It's a mixed blessing."

"She must be fit to be tied," Dempsey commented, then grimaced. "Sorry."

Clawson chuckled. "Oh, she's plenty pissed," he stated. "Still, in light of how her husband died, and the fortune he's left her, she's taking it pretty well."

* * * * *

Tiberius J. Muck looked out over the seventh fairway of the East Course. Standing at the tee, he looked down upon the verdant expanse in awe and wonder. I own it, he thought, because no one had yet been able to rally enough of a challenge to unseat his team from the tournament's throne.

His smile was almost childlike in its joy.

The team of Muck, Baxter, Pfunke, and Howe was the undisputed tournament champions seven years running. Even before that, they never placed any lower than third, but that had never been a great consolation to Muck and the others.

"If you don't play to win," he'd said on more than one occasion, "don't bother playing...and stay out of my way."

He was as dedicated a competitor as one could find, and the prospect of losing never entered his mind.

His drive went straight down the fairway.

"That's gotta be two-seventy" Howe stated, a hint of awe in his voice.

"Two-eighty," corrected Muck. "I don't hit 'em much better than that."

Caligula, sitting by the golf carts, watched as the ball came to a stop. He whined plaintively, anxious to run and retrieve the ball, but uncertain still what was expected of him.

He looked back at his master and chuffed.

"You stay right there, Cali," Muck commanded.

The dog had turned out to be less of an asset than he had originally hoped, but Muck was not one to give up on something, especially when he felt someone else was getting one over on him. Like Dempsey and his little fucking dog. That mutt would be a snack for Cali, and not much of one at that, and if he could figure out some way to make that happen he would.

There didn't seem to be much need for that though, even with the death of the Ice Cream King; they were in the lead by seven strokes with four weeks left to play. Dempsey and his crew weren't playing well enough to win. No, he reasoned, there's no need to take the dog out, but it would be a nice punctuation to winning the tournament.

Baxter swung at the ball, a hurried, jerky motion that sent his drive twenty yards to the left and deep into the grass.

"That was my fault," Muck stated. "I was talking."

Pfunke looked questioningly at his partner. No one had said a word. And that, thought Pfunke, is exactly what I'm going to do.

Baxter shrugged, teed up another ball, and managed a longer drive, though it did still go left.

"Damn," cursed Baxter.

"Not to worry," Muck said. He smiled at the young man with the male model good looks. Every move the man made, Muck thought, was like a pose for a fashion magazine. Even his golf swing, as ineffective as it was, looked like something from a pro's highlight reel.

Picture perfect. That was the absolute best description of Jauncy Baxter. The man was picture perfect. And like a picture he was two dimensional, with a depth that could be measured with a micrometer.

But far from being a problem, Baxter was the perfect team member; he looked like he knew what he was doing, and never argued about the rules. He deferred to Muck on everything.

Pfunke's drive, though not as far as Muck's, was also in the middle of the fairway.

Cali, again, chuffed.

"Not now, Cali. Stay!"

Howe stepped up and teed his ball. The non-descript man had a standard, set routine he went through with each shot, an annoying sequence of superstitious gestures that would put a baseball player to shame.

The little man would rest his club head on the ground, slowly gripping his club one finger at a time. He'd then pick the club head off the ground and raise it over his head, staring at it as though he'd never seen it before in his life. Once satisfied that the club was, in fact, his own, he'd swing it, from side to side, exactly three times. Any more or less, Muck knew from experience, and Howe would be forced to begin again.

Once relaxed with his swing, Howe would then place the club head behind the ball. Once placed, he'd adjust his feet. This adjustment, while a critical step in Howe's pre-swing routine, was a total mystery to anyone who'd ever played with the man.

Howe's foot placement appeared to be as random as a winning lottery number. On some shots his feet were too close and on others they were spread too wide. Sometimes, the left foot would be forward, sometimes the right would be forward. One would turn out on one swing, and then turn in on the next. There were times when the others wondered that he could hit the ball at all, given how he was standing, much less control its flight. But whatever he did with his feet, once set, no matter how awkward, he would start his swing and, without fail, send his shot as straight as an arrow.

Pfunke shook his head. "How does he do it?"

"Don't ask," Muck cautioned. "If he starts thinking about it he'll screw it up."

As they moved to the carts, Caligula became excited. The muscled Doberman sensed his time was coming.

"Your dog sure does like golf," Baxter observed.

"Cali likes the great outdoors."

Muck stood over his dog, unsure of what to think. No matter how hard he tried to teach the mutt, Caligula seemed unable to grasp the basic concept of ball spotting. He invariably picked the ball up, or nosed it, none of which mattered unless someone was watching. That had happened a few times and had cost the team strokes. He's beaten the dog soundly for those mistakes, discipline that Muck knew was critical to the dog's education. He wasn't about to let Cali get in the way of winning the Van Courtland Trophy.

"You be a good boy, Cali," he said. "Go on."

The Doberman was off like a thoroughbred out of the gate. Long, fluid strides carried the ebon canine down the fairway.

"He sure does like to run," Howe observed, slipping his driver into his bag.

"Yeah," Pfunke agreed. "It's a wonder he hasn't run off."

"What do you mean?" Muck turned on his partner. "Are you saying he should run off?"

"Not at all," Pfunke countered. The spindly man wasn't necessarily cowed by Muck, but when the bigger man got in one of his moods, and they could descend at anytime, anywhere, he was unpleasant to be around. "I meant that a lot of other dogs have run off."

"I heard that a couple ran off yesterday."

"I heard the same thing."

In fact, the runaway golf dogs seemed to be almost as popular a topic of discussion as the tournament.

Since the beginning of the tournament more than a dozen dogs, of all sizes and breeds, had run away from their owners. There was a general consensus amongst the owners that the dogs would come back when they got hungry or tired. McTavish shared that opinion, and was willing to ignore them unless they became a major impediment to the tournament.

"Cali won't run away," Muck declared, reassuring his golf partners. "He likes the good life too much."

The four men laughed as they sped off in their carts.

Muck and Howe, sharing a cart, sped off down the center of the fairway. Pfunke and Baxter angled off to the left, towards an area of thick grass and high bushes. Cali had hurried off in the general direction of Baxter's shot.

"I sure hope that dog has some idea where it went," Baxter stated, "'cause I don't."

As they neared the area where Baxter's ball had landed, Caligula came bounding out from behind a thick bush with Baxter's ball in his mouth.

Both men looked quickly around. With the exception of Muck and Howe, there was no one else in sight.

"Put it down, Cali." Baxter spoke softly as he left the cart. He slowly approached the dog. "Be a good boy and drop the ball."

Caligula let the ball fall from his mouth. It bounced on a tuft of grass, then rolled into a small declivity under the grass.

"Good dog," Pfunke said, silently cursing the roll of the ball. He looked at Baxter. "What do we do?"

Baxter shrugged. "I don't know?"

"I think," came a thick Highland's brogue from behind an adjacent bush, "you'll need to take a penalty stroke."

McTavish stepped smoothly from behind a nearby bush, his sporran swaying as he walked.

"I couldn't help but notice that your dog picked up your ball."

"He's not my dog," Baxter corrected, hopefully.

"But it is your ball."

Baxter squatted down and carefully pulled the thick grass aside. It was his ball.

"What's the problem here?" Muck and Howe, having spotted McTavish, hurried over.

"There's no problem," clarified McTavish, patting Cali on the head. "The dog moved the ball. Under USGA Rule 18-2, that's a penalty stroke."

"Are you sure," Muck challenged.

The dour Scot nodded, his eyes fixed firmly on Muck.

"Absolutely," said the Scot.

It wasn't unusual for McTavish to wander the course during the day, keeping an eye on things. He hadn't targeted Muck and the others for special scrutiny, but he wasn't surprised to find that they might be playing fast and loose with the rules.

He'd been around golf all his life and there was one thing about the game and the players that he knew with absolute certainty; no matter how good a player was, he was not going to win consistently. Even the pros experienced dry spells and slumps, barely finishing in the money much less taking home top prize.

It was because of that simple fact of the game that McTavish had suspected something wasn't quite right with Muck's game. The Scot, like most golfers, didn't want to believe one of their own would callously flaunt the rules for personal gain. On the other hand, there was a stubborn streak of pragmatism running through the man that questioned the probability of any one team winning the Van Courtland Cup in back to back tournaments. It challenged his faith in a supreme being that a team could win seven years in a row.

"So, I guess, along with the stroke, we'll need to take another penalty to get the ball out from under the grass?"

Muck pointed to where the ball rested.

McTavish shook his head. "You can have relief from the lie, since it was the dog that put it there." He gave Caligula another pat. "Wouldn't be sportin' to punish you twice for one mistake."

"Thanks," Howe said, his courtesy rewarded with an angry growl from Muck.

McTavish turned and walked away.

"Be sure to take the stroke, gentlemen," the Scot called over his shoulder. "I'll be sure to check the cards later today."

Muck scowled at Caligula. The dog had screwed up too many times. This last mistake made it nearly impossible now for them to be creative with their scoring. McTavish would scrutinize all of their cards from here on out. Worse, because the little man in the kilt had appeared from nowhere, it would be impossible to know when they were being observed. That made the use of 'foot adjustments' and 'hand wedges' no longer a viable remedy for bad lies, not to mention some of the other techniques they sometimes used to lower their score.

"Dammit," Pfunke muttered. He angrily grabbed his hat and threw it to the ground. In his pique, however, he also grabbed his hairpiece. Both hat and toupee lay accusingly at his feet.

Caligula sniffed guardedly at the clump of hair.

"This shouldn't be a problem," Howe cautioned. "We've been playing well this year. And we're still ahead."

Muck nodded. "Yeah," he said, "we should be all right, but that was a very stupid thing to do."

His eyes narrowed. His hand moved to his belt buckle and eased the belt from around his waist.

Muck looked at his dog as he doubled the leather into a strap.

"Don't do that, T.J.," Baxter asked. "Not again."

"Cali needs a lesson," Muck answered.

The Doberman, sitting obediently before his master, began to quiver.

"Cut it out, T.J." Howe stepped between Muck and his dog. "It's not a big deal."

"Get out of my way, Charles."

"Put your belt back on, T.J. Leave the dog alone."

"Yeah, T.J.," Pfunke agreed. He picked up his hat and hair. As best he could he put the two back on his head. It looked as though a baby otter was trying to hide under the brim of his cap. "Cali didn't mean anything. Hell, we've been lucky. He's moved lots of balls."

"I said, get out of my way."

Baxter stepped into the fray. "You can't do this anymore," he said. "You can't beat your dog. Not around me."

Muck's face turned beet red. "I can," he hissed, bulling his way into his buddies. He raised the belt high over his head to strike. "And I will."

A low, ululating howl issued from the stand of trees on the far side of the fairway. It was joined by another voice, closer than the first, and slightly higher in pitch. That one was joined. Then a fourth. And then there were too many to distinguish. And they were all around the foursome.

The four men froze in what would appear to a casual onlooker as a struggle for a belt.

They looked nervously around. There were no dogs in sight, but the howling continued.

Cali looked around anxiously. He was no longer shaking. Whatever the others were communicating, he understood and was comforted.

He raised his head majestically and added his voice to the chorus.

"Cali," Muck commanded, "stop it."

The Doberman ignored his master.

"Look." Baxter pointed towards the fairway.

Sitting next to Muck's golf cart was a large, dirty white Samoyed. The dog, head cocked back, was howling towards the clear, blue sky, unaffected, it seemed, by the heat or humidity.

The Samoyed stopped howling. One by one, the other voices went quiet, the resulting silence frighteningly loud.

"What the..." Howe took a step towards the fairway. Behind him, Caligula began a throaty growl, his intent clear. The non-descript man stopped in his tracks.

All four men turned to face a snarling, hackled Doberman Pincer.

"What's wrong with your dog, Muck?"

"I don't know," he answered, "but you should have let me beat him."

"Just don't anybody move," Baxter warned, his eyes wide in terror.

It was an unnecessary caution.

In the fairway, the Samoyed barked twice.

Caligula, eyes still on Muck, answered with his own barks. Cautiously, the Doberman moved around the men. Once clear, he trotted out to the Samoyed, not bothering to look back.

"Cali," Muck called, "come back here."

The dog ignored him. Instead, the Samoyed and the Doberman went nose to nose, a cautious greeting between two strangers. Satisfied that they were no threat to each other, the two dogs, in an ancient canine ballet, positioned themselves to examine each other's butts.

"Isn't that cute," Pfunke observed. "Cali has a new friend."

"Shut up, Barney." Muck watched as his pet and the other dog became acquainted. It wasn't like Cali to take to another dog so quickly. Hell, he thought, it wasn't like his dog to take to another dog, period. It wasn't like Cali to growl and snarl, either, so he had no idea what was going on.

On the fairway, the two dogs completed their introductions. They capered briefly, then the white dog started off for the woods on the far side of the fairway.

Caligula watched as the Samoyed moved off. The Doberman barked after his new friend. The Samoyed stopped, turned, and barked a response.

The Doberman looked over his shoulder at Muck and the others. After a brief pause, the dog ran to the parked golf cart, leaned down, then ran after the Samoyed.

The two dogs disappeared into the woods.

"What was that all about," wondered Baxter.

"I don't know," Muck answered, "but the bastard took my ball."

* * * * *

"Did you hear that?" Pearsall looked off in the distance.

"Sounds like dogs." Dempsey stepped away from his shot. Whether Pearsall had said anything or not, the baying was distraction enough. "A lot of dogs."

"A damn Baskerville convention, by the sounds of it." Clawson shot a nervous glance towards the woods on either side of the fairway. "You think we're okay out here."

"No telling," Verdu answered.

Pearsall, sitting next to Arnie P., looked quickly around, casually draping his arm protectively around Arnie P. The dog shuddered nervously, licking his lips loudly.

"Don't worry, little buddy," he said. "I'll watch out for you."

"You know," Clawson started, "I've been hearing stories about these dogs."

"Me, too," Verdu added. "Some of the dogs just up and ran off."

The howling diminished, then increased, but seemed to be coming no nearer.

"How many dogs?" Pearsall stepped from the cart and grabbed his putter. The shortest club in his bag, he figured he could use it to good effect in close quarters.

Clawson shrugged. "I heard a dozen."

"I heard two dozen." Verdu eyed the distant line of trees. Movement in the shadows had drawn his attention. Nothing now, and he wasn't sure there had been anything other than a bird or a squirrel. "This whole dog thing is giving me the willies."

"Relax, Vince." Dempsey studied his smaller friend. "The dogs that ran off are domesticated, as far from their feral heritage as we are from the trees."

"I'm not so sure," Clawson commented. He tried to clear his mind as he prepared his shot, a one hundred and fifty yard short iron to the green. The others were closer to the green, but if he hit this well, he'd be on first.

Dempsey continued. "The dogs that ran off are taking a little holiday. When they get hungry and tired, they'll show up at the clubhouse, or at some house in the area. This is probably the only chance most of them have had to spend time with other dogs."

"The rumor is that they're running in a pack."

"A pack? A pack is just the easiest way to define a group of dogs that travel together. In fact, a dog pack is a tight knit group of animals that hunt and stalk in concert. They've spent months, no years, bonding. They are an organized unit with a leader and a clearly defined hierarchy.

"What we're dealing with is a bunch of dogs that are just running around together. They can't be organized. They haven't been together that long."

Pearsall wasn't sure. He looked down at Arnie P., glad that they were all together and not spread out in the fairway.

Clawson's ball flew straight and true, a high arch that seemed to float across the sky.

"Beautiful shot, Rex." Dempsey watched with undisguised admiration.

The ball landed at the edge of the green, then rolled to within six feet of the hole.

"I smell birdie," teased Pearsall.

The four men laughed. Their laughter died as they watched a half dozen dogs emerge from the trees surrounding the green.

From where they were standing, the four men couldn't clearly distinguish the types of dogs, but they could see a large, dirty white dog and a large, muscular black and tan dog standing shoulder-to-shoulder in front of the other dogs.

The two lead dogs stared at the four men as one of the other dogs scooted forward and picked up Clawson's ball in its jaws.

Arnie P. whined, then made a move to leave the cart. Pearsall grabbed the dog's collar.

"You stay put, Arnie. They don't look all that friendly."

The small dog pulled against his collar, anxious to retrieve his friend's ball. After three attempts, he relented and sat quietly on the seat.

The two lead dogs threw their heads back and howled, their voices joined by others, both nearby and distant.

The canine chorus was short and pointed. As quickly as the dogs had appeared, they vanished.

"Well I'll be..." Dempsey whispered.

"I don't know as much about dogs as you do, Travis," Verdu confessed, "but they seemed pretty well organized to me."

* * * * *

There were over three dozen balls stolen by marauding canines that day. In some cases, as reported by angry and frustrated golfers, their balls hadn't stopped rolling before they were picked up and trotted off into the woods. According to the reports, many delivered to McTavish in breathless, indignant tones, the dogs had moved with the certainty and formation of a military operation, the lead dog flanked by two or three other dogs, with one more standing sentinel at the edge of the woods or high grass. The dogs had moved quickly, with purpose. Once the ball was snatched, the dogs vanished, the only proof of their passing were the sputtering, penalized golfers left in their wake.

McTavish was sympathetic, but the rules were the rules. The decision had been made early on to allow dogs in foursomes and on the course, he reminded all who were now arguing for some relief. It is axiomatic that rules don't change in the middle of a game.

"And we'll not be changing the rules now."

For some reason, still a mystery to McTavish, otherwise sober, mature, intelligent men and women of business, politics, and the arts all believed that their family pets would make a difference in their tournament play. It was ludicrous, of course, and what his mother would have referred to as 'the ash man's folly.' In truth, he'd never understood the majority of his mother's sage aphorisms, but they had always been colorful and entertaining.

True, it was the height of folly for intelligent people to place their hopes and faith in their dogs, but the game was different in America.

An entire industry had grown up around creating devices to help the golfer improve their game; special clubs, special club handles and grips, putters designed by NASA engineers, balls with special dimples, balls with special paint textures, gloves for cold, gloves for wet, gloves for heat, gloves for Cinco de Mayo, hats with every logo imaginable, specially designed sunglasses, and golf shoes with special spikes designed by NASA engineers. And that was before getting to the truly bizarre equipment; headgear that helped the golfer keep his head down, special arm wraps that kept the golfer from bending his arm during the back swing, specially designed golf tees...probably the product of a group of NASA engineers...that ensured straighter drives, and monoculars that measured distances to the green, as well as electronic score cards. A golfer could easily spend their children's college fund on special equipment, clubs, carts, clothes, and training before ever setting foot on a golf course.

Quite a world away from where the wiry Scot had grown up with the game. He'd had his bag of clubs, a few balls, and that was it. It was a much quicker game back then, much faster than the modern game. A player hit the ball, walked to the ball, then hit it again. No preamble, no stroke ritual, no cart to park, and no dithering over club selection.

Yes, he thought, a much faster game. A much cheaper game, too.

And no dogs.

When Dempsey first broached the idea of using his dog as a spotter, McTavish had almost let his reserved Scottish nature slip. The man needed glasses, his vanity be damned. But as he'd thought about it, the idea of dogs spotting balls appealed to a streak of whimsy that ran deep through his Scottish soul. It would never work, of course. He'd known that instantly, but the idea had the virtue of never having been tried. The Scot snorted happily as he mentally composed his letters to the USGA and the Royal and Ancient Golf Club at St. Andrews. He almost laughed out loud as he imagined the incredulity on the faces of the rule makers.

McTavish hadn't anticipated that the tournament outcome would vary greatly, with or without the dogs. In truth, though, he hadn't anticipated that dogs would run off, either, or that they would begin stealing golf balls. On this one day alone, he thought, he'd had three eyewitness accounts of dogs stealing balls in play. He'd heard a dozen other complaints of lost balls where canine intervention was suspected, but no dogs had been seen.

It was an annoying development, he understood, but the tournament was soon over, and the great dog experiment would end, never to be tried again. At that point, the missing dogs would be rounded up and sent home. Until then, the tournament would continue.

* * * * *

Josh looked nervously around as he walked from the parking lot to the east side driving range of the Van Courtland Glen Country Club. Even with a golf bag on his shoulder and a Nike ball cap on his head, the undercover Uffie was certain that everyone he passed knew him to be a fraud. Worse, he was convinced that they knew his true mission at the club.

The plan was simple. He was to go to the club and blend in, gaining as much information as he could about the layout of the club and course. Leigh was good at making plans, but lacking any native athletic ability, and never having held a golf club in his life, Josh wasn't quite as confident in his own ability to pull it off.

And yet, here he was, making his way to the driving range at one of the premiere golfing facilities on the east coast of the United States, trying to pass himself off as a golfer.

He followed the signs marked 'Driving Range – East', staying on the well-tended red brick path as it wended its way up to, then around, the stately white club house. It was a huge building, easily as large as the campus administration building, and as grand as any southern estate this side of Tara. It lent majesty to the surroundings, if not the game, and Josh felt a stirring at the base of his spine.

From the surroundings alone he could well sense the attraction of the game.

"You lost, lad?"

A small, wiry man in a green skirt and matching floppy hat stood in front of the young college student.

"I'm looking for the driving range," Josh said, haltingly, still not sure about the man standing before him.

McTavish eyed the young man, sensing immediately a person unfamiliar with the game.

"The driving range, you say?"

Josh nodded.

"That would be the area immediately to your left."

McTavish tilted his head in the direction of the range.

Not twenty feet away was the wide patch of close cut grass of the range. Golfers of all shapes and sizes were practicing their swings and expanding their vocabularies. The balls sailed, with varying degrees of accuracy, out to the wide-open field.

Josh looked at the field, then back at McTavish. There was something compelling about the man's outfit; high, green socks rising proudly from the worn golf shoes, the briefest hint of flesh before the hem of the heavy woolen skirt came into view. And what was that leather pouch for, the young man wondered, only then realizing that there were probably no pockets in the skirt.

"You've never seen manly attire, I take it?"

"What?"

"You're staring at m' kilt, lad."

"I'm sorry," Josh answered, still staring.

"As well you should be," the Scot stated. "Laddie," he began, reaching out and tilting the boy's head up to meet his eyes, "you keep eyeing me like that, and me and you'll be takin' a trip to Achiltibuie."

Josh had no idea what that meant, or if he'd heard clearly what the man had said, but there was no mistaking the mild threat carried in the tone.

McTavish smiled, a rare sight. He liked the stringy haired lad who smelled faintly of macadam. He seemed quiet, soft spoken...a rarity among the youth of today.

"Your father's a member?"

"Yes," Josh lied. McTavish nodded, seeing the answer for what it was.

"How long have you been a player," asked the Scot.

Josh reddened. "I've never played before."

McTavish nodded sagely. "It's best to start when you're young. Come on."

The wiry man turned toward the range, leading the tyro golfer to an empty square of turf overlooking the expanse of open field.

The Uffie followed obediently, bewildered and a bit concerned. He was at the club to collect information. He certainly didn't need the attention of the kilted man who, judging by the greetings and waves of the others on the range, was well known at the club.

"Set the clubs down, boy." McTavish directed, handing Josh a small, brass token about the size of a quarter. "Run up to The Monster and get a bucket of balls."

"The Monster?"

"The ball machine," the Scot explained. "It's a temperamental beast with a mind of its own. You'll get your balls," he assured the young man, "but you'll either have to sweet talk it or put the wood to it."

'Put the wood to it?"

"You'll find a well-worn wooden club leaning against the machine. If talking to it won't do the trick, stand well clear of the snout when you hit it with the club."

"Why not just get it fixed?"

"Tried," the wiry man answered. "Tried everything. Can't be fixed. Just managed." He laughed. "Quite a draw, though. Most everyone's heard of The Monster."

Josh ambled off in the direction the Scot had indicated, uncertain what was next. This wasn't what he'd expected, nor was The Monster.

The legendary ball machine was nothing more than a very large corrugated metal box, about three times the size of a kitchen refrigerator, in desperate need of repainting. The sides of the machine seemed to be in fairly decent shape, save for the paint that hung from random bare spots like skin from a burn victim, with the whole thing being sheltered somewhat by overhanging limbs from an adjacent tree. In any other setting, The Monster would be nothing other than a major eyesore. Here, next to the driving range and close proximity to the back door of the clubhouse kitchen, it seemed to be in its element.

The novice golfer, unsure of his next move, stepped to one side as another golfer stepped up to get balls.

"You're a lucky boy," commented the brightly attired man. He moved confidently and took a battered wire basket from a rack of baskets to the side of the machine.

"I'm sorry?"

"McTavish." The man gestured towards the Scot standing motionless at the range. "He's going to give you a lesson."

"Lesson?"

The man nodded. He placed the basket into a recess at the front of the machine. The basket nestled snuggly into a slot just beneath a worn metal chute. The chute swayed from side to side as he pulled his hand away. Producing a brass token identical to Josh's, the man inserted it in a slot on the top of the machine and waited.

The machine gurgled once, then fell silent.

"Damn," the man hissed, looking at Josh and shaking his head in disgust.

He waved Josh to the side as he picked up a scarred and gouged bat leaning against the machine. Satisfied that the boy was clear, the man slammed the board into the front of the machine.

Judging from the badly dented exterior, beating The Monster was a routine occurrence.

The man kept hitting the machine until the low gurgling resumed.

"Fore!" The man's voice rang out loudly, scaring Josh with its suddenness, and drawing the attention of everyone on the range. All heads turned towards The Monster.

With one last swing of the board, the machine belched and shot a golf ball violently from the end of the ball chute. The ball was a low screamer. It hit the ground twenty feet from the golfer on the range, then took an erratic hop towards an elderly man whose surprised squeal was quickly followed by an angry stream of invective after the ball bashed into his right calf.

"That's going to bruise," the man stated. He waved to the victim. "Sorry, Frank."

The old man waved and limped to a nearby bench. Other golfers came to his side to offer aid and solace.

With that out of its system, a steady stream of range balls poured harmlessly into the waiting wire basket.

"Yup, a lesson." The man continued on as though nothing bizarre had happened. He reached down and grabbed the wire basket of balls. "You related?"

Josh shook his head. "I've never met the man."

"Then he's taken a shine to you," the man commented. "Take full advantage of the kindness he's showing you. You'll never have a better teacher."

Josh approached the ball machine fearfully. He put the wire basket under the ball chute, inserted the token McTavish had given him, then stood back. Without preamble or fanfare, range balls tumbled into the basket. He breathed a sigh of relief.

Returning with the basket of balls, Josh again considered the small Scot. Other than the unique attire, there seemed nothing special about him.

"Right," the Scot said. "Now set the balls down and take a club."

"Which one?"

"It's of no consequence to me, lad. You'll be the one using it."

How do I get out of this, he thought, taking the nearest club from the bag? He needed to be spying, collecting information. Wolfe wouldn't be at all happy if he came back empty handed.

"Quit gathering wool, boy," McTavish said. "You've got an ancient sport to learn and only a lifetime to learn it."

* * * * *

The tall, slender man in the new polo shirt and crisp ball cap walked with a leisurely gate through the large greeting hall of the clubhouse. He looked innocently around the richly appointed surroundings, taking in every detail, his long ponytail tucked up under his cap. Tourists and curious local residents were not uncommon at Van Courtland Glen...their visits were encouraged as part of a 'good neighbor' policy...but Leigh Wolfe knew that people's memories picked up odd bits of information...like a ponytail on a man...so when the questioning started he didn't want that tidbit showing up on the police reports.

The golf facility, or what he'd seen of it, was truly grand, and he was not inured to such splendor. In his younger days he would have been scandalized that such wealth could rest in the hands of an idle few while so many around the world struggled through life with so little. Tragic, to be sure, but age, experience, and knowledge had taught him that very few of the wealthy started that way. They'd worked long and hard to achieve their goals, often making great personal sacrifices, rarely achieving success on their first try. And they tended, too, as a group, to be generous with their money, and time, helping others less fortunate than themselves. They weren't saints...far from it...but they also weren't the underlying cause, or the only salvation, for the starvation, death, disease, and famine throughout the world, as so many bleeding hearts believed. He'd learned the hard way, after years of protesting against what he had idealistically viewed as fathomless greed, and for what he'd believed was the only enlightened path to follow, that governments, not the wealthy, were to blame for the suffering of their people. The dilemma for the idealist was in the conflict that arose when the government, supposedly in place to protect the weakest in the group, cared only for itself. Governments were as different as night and day, but treating them all the same, holding all accountable for the wrongs of a few, only created confusion and frustration.

Wolfe peeked into a large banquet hall.

Yes, he thought, governments were very different. As he'd grown and matured, he'd come to that realization, and he'd come to value the fact that he lived under a strong democratic system of government that offered its citizens freedoms and protections unheard of in most of the rest of the world. It was these freedoms that allowed Wolfe and others to pursue their dreams and passions, such as animal rights though, in truth, he hadn't felt passionately about animal rights for some time.

As one of the original founders of UFLACADAC, Leigh Wolfe had single handedly organized, coordinated, publicized, and grown a grass roots animal rights group into a world-wide, money making special interest organization. Within ten years of its founding, UFLACADAC had established a national headquarters in Washington, D.C. The office had been small and cramped, not unlike his Fredericksburg office, but it had represented the success a well-organized social cause could achieve. Granted, some of the techniques used to achieve that success were questionable, not just legally but ethically, but vandalism and destruction in the cause of animal rights was not a vice, and lawfulness in the face of vivisection was no virtue, or so his tracts had proclaimed.

The more aggressive, lawless UFLACADAC faction had been dubbed ARF, the Animal Revolutionary Front, and had been dedicated to the more 'in-your-face' sorts of civil actions. During the late 70's and early 80's, ARF claimed responsibility for over 100 acts of vandalism ranging from simple property defacement to arson. ARF had been responsible for the Sioux City, Iowa rabbit infestation and was the prime suspect in the Butte, Montana trucking terminus fire. Across the United States and in major cities in Europe, the ARF acronym appeared spray painted on walls, printed in anonymous circulars on every major college campus, and listed in the files of most major metropolitan police forces and the FBI. ARF achieved an infamy out of all proportion to its size, and Wolfe had been heartened by the success achieved by a small, faceless group he'd organized and trained.

ARF had been his brainchild, the smaller, more energetic, more focused arm of the animal rights movement.

In the early days, UFLACADAC and ARF were part of the same package in most everyone's mind, a perception that had hurt neither. As the movement had grown, however, and as UFLACADAC became more mainstream, their association with a violent, borderline criminal faction became problematic. By the late 80's, UFLACADAC had grown into a multinational concern with a president and a board of directors, and a sizable, not-for-profit bottom line. With an understanding of what there was to lose, Wolfe had been forced out of his leadership position.

To say that Wolfe had been angry and bitter was like referring to a force five hurricane as 'a little blow.' His anger had been limitless, and his bitterness grew with each passing day, but he had not survived hundreds of covert acts of civil disobedience and destruction by being headstrong and precipitous.

He'd accepted his exile with outward magnanimity and settled just south of D.C. in Fredericksburg. He'd taken over the local UFLACADAC office and grown it into a regional volunteer center.

He'd played along for years, towing the organizational line of 'peaceful protest' in support of 'our animal brethren and sisteren.' He had not executed any ARF actions against any reasonable targets after leaving the national office. He had hoped, in fact, that the public awareness of ARF and its activities would fade with time, memories of the splinter group fading like the wisps of steam from a mug of hot coffee. In that way, he'd reasoned, the next ARF action…and there would be one…would have that much more of an impact.

Looking around the golf course, Leigh Wolfe spotted numerous targets of opportunity. He allowed himself a brief smile. This would be the revenge he'd wanted for so many years. His cold blue eyes scanned the facility. His patience had paid off.

He'd done some research and learned that the Van Courtland Glen Country Club was a nationally known facility, with some powerful and influential members. Because the course was open to the public, even in a limited capacity, the club had skirted much of the public opprobrium reserved for exclusive, private clubs. As near as Wolfe was able to learn, Van Courtland Glen Country Club was a respected, respectable establishment.

Until now.

Having pets was bad enough, something UFLACADAC strongly opposed, but using them as golf slaves was beyond the pale. Most people were ambivalent about the sport of golf, but they wouldn't be quite as indifferent once the truth was known.

A cold smirk danced across his lips.

ARF would strike again, linking itself with UFLACADAC once more and forever. By striking against such a well-known, well-connected target, UFLACADAC, even with its most fervent denials, would not be able to weather the firestorm that was coming. Especially once he made clear the on-going link between UFLACADAC and ARF.

They'd made a terrible mistake when they'd pushed him out. They were soon to learn just how serious a mistake it had been.

Wolfe exited the building, stepping onto a veranda with a panoramic view of three neatly manicured fairways. Everything else aside, he thought, it is truly a lovely facility.

He rounded the corner of the building, his eyes constantly moving, taking in everything. At the driving range he noticed a large, battered metal machine. That might be useful, he thought, noting the young man at the range.

"Joshua?"

As Wolfe approached, the college student turned.

"Leigh. Hi."

"Josh," the older man asked, "what are you doing?"

"Practicing a draw," he said, excitedly. "Watch this."

The young man swung at the ball as though he'd been playing the game his entire life. The ball left the mat with a sharp 'thwack,' angling to the right, then coming back to the left in a gentle arch.

Wolfe watched the ball, his expression neutral.

"See," Josh explained, "it goes right to left, but not a lot. Too much and that's a hook."

"So?"

"Well, you don't want a hook. A draw is good, especially on a leftward fairway. A hook's only good for scaring other golfers or for getting rid of balls you don't want."

"I didn't know you were a golfer."

Josh reddened. "I'm not, but McTavish says I'm a natural."

"That's good," Wolfe said. His eyes narrowed angrily. "But did you find out anything that will help us? That *is* why we're here, remember?"

"I remember," the boy nodded. "I just got carried away with my golf lesson…"

"…lesson?"

"It didn't cost anything."

Wolfe took a step closer to the college student.

"We're supposed to be finding out what's going on here," he whispered. "This club is exploiting animals for human enjoyment."

Josh scratched his head. "Well, I asked Mac…"

"…Mac?"

"McTavish. I asked him about the dogs."

"You asked?"

Josh shrugged. "Why not? They're pretty much all over the place."

Wolfe turned and, for the first time, noticed that, yes, there were quite a few dogs at the club. Most were on leashes, though there were one or two roaming free. There was one, he noticed, some sort of terrier, sitting in the shadow of the building, watching the machine as it whined, coughed, and then spat a tumble of white balls into a wire basket.

"Mac told me that this was just an experiment. They won't be having dogs on the course after Labor Day."

"Why Labor Day?"

"That's the end of the tournament."

Wolfe nodded. Labor Day. What was it he'd read on one of the bulletin boards?

"Good job, Josh." He patted the boy's shoulder. "Keep practicing."

Wolfe turned and headed back towards the clubhouse. If the dogs were going away, his window of opportunity was limited. He would have to act quickly.

* * * * *

The Australian terrier panted in the heat, even though he was in the shadows. The Dog Days of August had moved in with a vengeance, but Fritz Bones Fizzles, as his master had dubbed him, was uncaring of the heat. His full attention was on the large, green, clattering box twenty feet away. Whatever it was held a treasure of the white things that were so important to his master. They were of no value to Fritz. They were as hard as rocks so they couldn't be chewed. They couldn't be eaten. And since they couldn't be eaten or chewed, there was no point in burying them, especially since they were everywhere. Still, they were important to his master.

He hadn't seen his master in a while. Were he to have a concept of time, he'd understand that almost three weeks had passed since he'd run off with the other dogs. He missed his master, the patting, the belly scratching, and the easy food on demand. But they were playing a game. Find the ball, hit the ball away. Find the ball, hit the ball away again. Fetch. Stay. Fetch. Fritz understood fetch. This was a bit different, but it was fun.

All the dogs were having fun. They'd collected all sorts of the white balls. They were easy to find. And the masters brought more every day. It was not a game Fritz understood, but he was fine playing it. Get the white balls.

And now that he'd found what appeared to be an unlimited source of the balls, the others should know.

Fritz moved from the shadows and sauntered slowly down the path towards the first tee of the North Course. He waited behind one of the large wheeled machines until the women had hit more balls away. Fritz was tempted to run after them, but now that he'd found the noisy box full of balls, there wasn't much point. Besides, once out of the shadows, it was hot.

Fritz Bones Fizzles made his way to a copse of trees to the right of the first fairway. From there he would make his way to the den.

* * * * *

Travis Dempsey stood at the sixth tee of the North Course, his mind dancing lightly from one subject to the next.

One week remained in the Van Courtland Glen annual golf tournament and his team had gained on the leader. Muck and his crew were still in first place, but the numbers had changed. Muck's seven-stroke lead over Dempsey had been cut to four strokes. It was anyone's tournament.

How Muck lost his commanding lead was the subject of much speculation. The members of Van Courtland Glen Country Club were too polite, at least publicly, to hazard an opinion on what had happened to the tournament front-runner, but privately the smart money was on Muck having been caught cheating. It was the only logical explanation for his steady slide in the standings. If true, no one expected the offending foursome to be banished from the tournament...it might prove embarrassing for the club...but they would be closely watched for the remainder of the tournament, and in all future tournaments. They were no less formidable in their play, Dempsey reasoned, but it was like confiscating the steroids from the East German team; they might still beat you, but it was no longer a foregone conclusion.

In fact, there were very few things about this year's tournament that were certain.

It had started innocently enough with Arnie P. Dempsey had certainly never anticipated that his simple request would mushroom into such an unmitigated, irredeemable cluster fuck. At last count, almost three dozen dogs had run off, trading domesticity for a feral existence in the rolling hills of Spotsylvania County, making the odd appearance to worry golfers and steal golf balls. Why they would take golf balls was a mystery; it was assumed the dogs had run off because they wanted nothing further to do with the game. Their reappearances to snatch the balls, sometimes before they'd stopped rolling, made no sense to anyone.

Thirty-some dogs constituted a pack, by anyone's definition, and while no one had seen all the dogs together, and no large group of dogs had threatened anyone, the thought of that many dogs running lose, without any human supervision or control, was unsettling. The Club had made some low-key inquiries with local animal control experts about what to do and what to expect. Dempsey knew this because he'd recommended the Club take that course of action as a hedge against any liability and potential lawsuits. He had offered his legal advice to the head of the membership committee, *pro bono*. It seemed the least he could do given the mess he had, unwittingly, created. He was sorry that the whole thing turned out so badly, but there was nothing to do now but prepare for possible outcomes and finish the tournament.

Which was just how a number of the tournament participants saw the situation…sort of.

As the dogs began disappearing, now dog-less tournament members approached McTavish for a ruling, lobbying for special dispensation. Since they no longer had their dogs, and others did, it was only fair, they argued, that they receive some special consideration. Unfortunately for them, McTavish was not inclined to listen to a bunch of whining players who, not two months earlier, had argued for the right to bring their dogs to the course. The irascible Scotsman had nipped the issue in the bud by suggesting that, without their dogs, their teams were no longer whole, and that the 'lost member' rule of the tournament might apply. Faced with disqualification, the troublesome members had vanished as quickly as their dogs, which resolved the issue of how the tournament would deal with the disappearance of a dog from a team, but not with the missing dogs themselves.

As for the missing dogs, well, the whole golf dog issue was no longer a Van Courtland Glen Country Club matter.

Driving up to the stone gates of the club entrance earlier, he'd been greeted by the sight of two dozen animal rights activists. They were a small, disorganized, ragtag group, and their slogans, painted hurriedly onto poster board, hadn't made much sense...'Don't Enslave the Unenslaveable!' one had cryptically commanded...but it was just the beginning. The crowd would grow and the slogans would get more focused. It was all just a matter of time.

"Are you going to hit the ball, Travis?"

Verdu, Clawson, Pearsall, and Arnie P. were lined up at the edge of the tee box. The three men were relaxed, their hands resting gently on their drivers.

Arnie P. sat quietly at the end of the row. He watched the ball on the tee, his ears turned forward and his head cocked to one side. He, too, was anxious for the game to continue.

Dempsey gave his friends a sheepish grin.

He looked out over the fairway, a wide, forgiving par four that was as straight as a plumb line and promised far better lies than his clients. The only danger lay in the trees lining either side of the fairway. The fairway was so wide, however, that the trees only came into play with a crippling slice or devastating hook.

He stepped up to the ball, eased into this stance, settled himself, then swung his driver with a slow, easy arch. The ball jumped from the tee and sailed straight down the middle of the fairway.

When the ball finished its roll, Dempsey's drive had traveled almost three hundred yards.

"Beautiful drive," Pearsall stated. "Someone ate his Wheaties this morning."

Verdu turned to Clawson. "With drives like that we shouldn't rush him?"

"Yes," Dempsey agreed, "you shouldn't rush me."

Clawson stepped into the box, teeing his ball.

Arnie P. started barking.

"I guess Arnie P. thinks it was a good drive, too." Pearsall looked down at the agitated Jack Russell.

The dog was standing, his hackles raised, his attention turned down the fairway.

"I don't think he's excited about the drive," Clawson corrected. He nodded his head toward the trees on the left of the fairway.

"Shit," Dempsey cursed. "Not again."

The three dogs trotted from the tree line out to Dempsey's ball. Playfully, they nosed it around, batting it between them.

"Look at the bright side," offered Verdu. "No matter how much they move it around, it's not a penalty."

"And maybe they'll move it closer to the hole," offered Clawson.

"Yeah," Dempsey sighed. "I feel much better knowing that."

Tiring of their game, the dog nearest the ball snatched it up and turned back to the tree line, flanked by the other two dogs.

Before anyone thought to move, Arnie P. was off like a shot, bounding down the fairway, his small legs springing him forward.

"Arnie. No!" Dempsey called after his dog, understanding, even as he did, his calls would be ignored.

"Let's go get him," Pearsall said. He dropped his club and turned towards the carts.

"Mitch," Dempsey called. "Wait."

"We've got to get him back."

"He'll be back," Dempsey said, hoping his voice didn't betray the doubt he felt.

"How can you be sure?" Pearsall stood by the cart, conflicted. He knew he'd never catch Arnie P. unless the dog wanted to be caught. On the other hand, he wasn't comfortable with his little friend out there, alone, with all those other dogs. "How do you know he'll come back?"

It was a good question. Dempsey didn't know his Jack Russell terrier would return, just as it had never occurred to him that Arnie P. would run off. Why now, he wondered. Why today? He had no good answer.

"He'll be back," he repeated, hoping to reassure his big friend. "He'll get hungry. He'll get tired. He'll be back."

Reassuring words he thought. He hoped. Arnie P. *would* eventually get hungry. *And* tired. But with two dozen other dogs out there, it was unlikely that his little friend would be lonely.

* * * * *

The state of Virginia is comprised of three distinct geological regions; the Tidewater, the Piedmont, and the Mountains and Valleys. On the east side of state, the Tidewater region, so named because of the Atlantic's tides that enter the Chesapeake Bay, and thus the four rivers whose wide mouths open to the bay; the Potomac, Rappahannock, York, and James.

On the western side of the state is the region of Mountains and Valleys. The Blue Ridge Mountains are there, as are the Appalachian Mountains. Nestled between the two ranges is the Shenandoah Valley, though the Shenandoah is simply the best known of the four major valleys of that region.

Between the mountains and valleys to the west and the coast on the east lies an area of geologic transition known as the Piedmont. The word, French for "foot of the mountains", accurately describes the subtle transformation from flat, arable land into the lush, rolling hills that undulate west towards the Blue Ridge. The hills, the valleys, the foliage, and rivers make this the perfect areas for homes, communities, businesses, and golf courses. It was on hundreds of acres of land in the Piedmont that the Van Courtland Glen Golf Course resided.

Unaware and uncaring of all this, as he was only distantly conscious of his master's voice calling to him, Arnie P. bounded through the woods after his ball-thieving rivals. It wasn't an ego thing for the wiry Jack Russell terrier, a concept as foreign to him as thievery or rivalry. It was a matter of loyalty, though the small dog would not have understood that concept, either. What Arnie P. understood was that the dogs he was chasing had taken his master's little white ball, and it was up to Arnie P. to get it back.

The Jack Russell followed the scent of the other dogs through the woods, catching glimpses of them through the trees. Occasionally, they would break cover of the trees and cross a fairway or a green, only to disappear again into another thicket of trees or high grass. Though their course zigzagged, it never varied much from a westerly direction.

Arnie P. would make up distance, closing the gap between himself and his master's ball, and then loose the trail. He would have to take time to backtrack and regain the scent, and then he was off again like a shot.

Soon, the small dog was beyond the confines of the golf course, a change that was less a conscious understanding than a sensual awareness. He stopped and looked back over his shoulder. Everything was new, strange, and so much different from what he knew. As he moved deeper into the woods, the heat and humidity abated slightly, the shadows offering true cooling and not just a dark promise. The terrain became steeper, rockier, a problem for many, but not for the small, sure-footed terrier.

A chorus of howls echoed from the steep hills before him. Deep, resonant ululating that sent birds winging from their perches, and froze the small, woodland creatures in their tracks.

Arnie P. whimpered softly, but continued on.

It didn't take him long to find the sheltered crevice in the side of the rocky outcropping. The fissure was redolent with the scent of dogs, many dogs, male and female. In the miasma he was able to recognize the scent of the dogs he'd been following. They had gone into the side of the hill. The Jack Russell disappeared into the black of the opening.

Little light followed him into the narrow passageway, and within a few yards he was in total darkness. His eyes, better suited for dark than human eyes, were still straining to see the path before him. His senses of smell and hearing, however, served him well. The scent of the others grew stronger the further he went, and the sound of the other dogs grew.

A faint light shone in front of him, a soft glow that clearly delineated a large gap a few yards further down the narrow passage.

The cavern Arnie P. discovered was not large, but it was spacious enough for the pack of dogs that had turned to greet him. He could see them all clearly, awash in a an odd light that seemed to radiate from the long, teeth-like structures that rose from the floor and hung from the high ceiling.

The males in the cave took tentative, threatening steps toward the small dog, other small dogs in the group yapping noisily. The females congregated behind the males, shielded from the unknown threat, but just as attentive as the males. None of the dogs made a move towards the wiry interloper.

From the shadowy heights of the cave, a large, sinewy black male made his way from ledge to ledge, descending to the floor of the cave. The male's black eyes, set above a brown, torpedo snout, considered the small white dog staring up at him.

Arnie P. looked away and remained still as the larger dog checked him out, snout to rectum. Perceiving no threat, the large dog made his way back up into the shadows, greeted there by a large, white furred bitch. Arnie P. sniffed the air. The leader's mate was pregnant.

The rest of the dogs relaxed and went about their business.

The Jack Russell began exploring the cave. Bones of small animals and birds littered the floor of the cave, as did random piles of excrement. In a small alcove off the main cave, Arnie P. found a small stream. He helped himself to cold, tangy water.

The main cave was the largest, and was where the pack congregated. Off the main cave were a number of other, smaller caves.

At the rear of one of these smaller caves was a crack in the rock. The small dog could see that the same soft light shone in whatever lay beyond, and he could tell by the scent that whatever lay beyond was frequented by the pack.

Arnie P. padded through the short tunnel and entered a high domed chamber. He stopped, sat down, and cocked his head in wonder.

Rising before him was a huge mound of golf balls. They glowed gently in the odd light from the rocks.

There was a narrow path that led up the side of the chamber that ended at a wide ledge directly above the pile of golf balls. On the ledge were the three dogs Arnie P. had been following. One held a ball in its mouth. His master's ball.

Arnie P. barked a warning, but the others ignored him.

The ball fell from the dog's jaws and dropped onto the top of the pile. A number of balls jumped, and some rolled down the sloped side of the mound.

The small dog approached the pile that towered above him. He sniffed each ball along the way.

TOURNAMENT'S END

Travis Dempsey drove through the stone gate of the Van Courtland Glen Country Club. He paid scant attention to the chanting protesters lining the far side of the road. They'd finally gotten organized and refined their message, their signs decrying the use of 'sport beasts', as well as signs vilifying pet ownership, period. Remembering the name of the group required more effort than he was willing to expend...the nonsensical, alphabablic string of vowels and consonants lent themselves to forgetfulness... and he flat out didn't care. He felt bad enough about his role in the golf dog fiasco, and awful about Arnie P. running off.

The Jack Russell was gone a week. Dempsey's best efforts to find the dog had proven fruitless, as had other members' efforts to find their missing pets. He'd even run into Muck, whose Doberman Pincer had run off several weeks earlier. Dempsey got the impression that Muck's concern had little to do with his missing dog and everything to do with keeping the family peace. That seemed to be the pervasive concern amongst the pet owners who, it turned out, should have left their pets at home. In that regard, he'd been fortunate. Donna, who'd never thought much of the idea to begin with, was sympathetic. She didn't blame him for Arnie P.'s disappearance.

"He's a dog," she'd stated. "I'm surprised the idea of 'summer camp' with a bunch of other dogs didn't occur to him sooner."

That notion brought a smile to his face, and hinted at what he hoped would be the final outcome, because hope was all any of them had at the moment.

The local animal control authorities investigated, but there was little they could do. There were no animals in need of control, and the occasional pilfering of golf balls didn't rate highly on their list of concerns.

The club had even gone so far as to hire a couple of professional trackers to hunt the dogs. After four days in the hilly woods of the Piedmont, the trackers confirmed that there were dogs out there, probably the missing pets, but were unable to get close enough to visually confirm anything.

It finally occurred to someone that the Piedmont was riddled with caves and caverns, affording a large pack of dogs the ability to vanish at will. The logical next step was to bring in spelunkers, but no one, especially not the governing body of Van Courtland Glen, wanted to go to that trouble and expense. From the club's standpoint the missing dogs weren't a big PR problem; pets had run away, and they were being picketed by animal rights activists. The dogs would eventually return, or not, and once they got the publicity they were after, the protesters would go away.

He parked his car.

The club's spokesperson, in a statement to a mildly interested press, spun the ill-conceived golf dog fiasco into a harmless, semi-serious method to add a little excitement to their annual golf tournament. The idea had been less of a success than they'd hoped, the spokesperson conceded, and would never be tried again, but trying new things was the American way, wasn't it?

That didn't make Dempsey feel any better. His dog was still missing. And as bad as he felt about it, Mitch felt worse.

The tall black man opened Dempsey's car door before the engine stopped.

"Any word?"

Travis looked up into the plaintive eyes of his friend.

Somewhere along the line, between the first day Arnie P. joined their team and the day he'd vanished into the shadowy woods in pursuit of those other dogs, Mitch Pearsall had developed a deep attachment for the feisty terrier. And Arnie P. had become quite fond of Pearsall.

"Nothing yet," answered Dempsey, stepping from his car.

"I thought he'd be back by now." Pearsall shook his head, disappointment chiseled on his face.

Dempsey was only too familiar with what Pearsall was feeling.

"It's going be okay, Mitch."

"I miss the little guy," the tall man admitted. "It's not the same golfing without him."

"It's the last round, Mitch." The two men made their way to the clubhouse. "Arnie P. would want you to go on."

Mitch shot his partner a worried look.

"I'm sure he's fine, but he isn't here right now." Dempsey was torn between his sincere sympathy for his friend and acknowledging the absurdity of the situation. "Look, if it will make you feel any better, I'll ask Vince to lick your head."

Pearsall laughed, relaxing.

"I'll be okay, Travis," he said, "but it's just not the same."

"I know," Dempsey agreed. "I know."

* * * * *

The banquet hall vibrated with a low, anticipatory hum. The tournament participants were at the end of a long trial. The final round would be played on this day, a beautiful, bright, steamy Saturday, the first Saturday in September, Labor Day Weekend.

Dempsey sat at a table close to the front of the room. Pearsall was next to him, both silent, in their own worlds. Funny, Dempsey thought. For most of the players in the room, today's round is meaningless. They're not in contention for any prize, much less the Cup.

He looked at the standing sheet in front of him. As expected, Muck's team was leading the pack, but only by two strokes. Close on their heels was Dempsey. Two strokes separated them from Muck, and three strokes put the Cup in their hands. Very manageable, he thought, considering how they'd been playing, and given that, by rule, tournament referees traveled with the top five teams on the final round. Stroke shaving was a virtual impossibility. And since the nearest team to Dempsey's was seven strokes back...ten strokes to win...the final round boiled down to the play of Dempsey and Muck.

Oddly, Dempsey was calmed by being in second place. Unless they totally screwed the pooch, they would do no worse than second overall. They could conceivably win the cup, but he pushed that thought from his mind.

Pearsall looked around the room. People were settling into their seats.

"I haven't seen Rex or Vince?"

Dempsey turned in his seat and scanned the room. "They'll be along."

McTavish, flanked by a group of referees, entered the room from a side door. All eyes were on the short man in the green kilt. As he approached the front of the room, Clawson and Verdu arrived, quietly taking their seats.

"You guys took your sweet time getting here."

Verdu nodded, turning his attention forward.

"Sorry," whispered Clawson.

McTavish raised a hand to quiet the room.

"Thank you," he said. The room noise dissipated instantly. The Scot looked appreciatively out over the room. "I'll not keep you long, knowin' as I do how anxious you are to complete your last round of the tournament."

Scattered applause broke out in the large room.

"This year, like all others, has been quite the event, though this one may be one for the record books."

Titters floated through the room.

"I can honestly say that until this year I thought I'd seen all there was to see in the golfing world. It just goes to show ya," he said, finding Dempsey in the crowd and winking, "that you *can* teach an old dog new tricks."

Dempsey reddened as appreciative laughter and applause filled the room.

"As you might have guessed, they'll be no dogs, old or otherwise, or tricks, new or not, going forward, but that doesn't change the unique nature of this year's tournament."

More applause.

"And just so you know," he added, "there'll be no dogs on today's round. Not that we've changed the rules, understand. Just that those owners who still have pets have decided to keep it that way."

Self-conscious laughter and applause filled the room.

McTavish waved the room to silence.

"So, where do we stand for the final day?" He examined a copy of the standings. "As has come to be the standard of the Van Courtland Glen tournament, Mr. Muck's foursome is atop the pack, ahead of the Dempsey foursome by two."

Some good natured, and not so good-natured boos, hoots, and catcalls rang out.

Muck rose from his seat, two tables behind Dempsey, and favored the attendees with an exaggerated bow.

McTavish acknowledged Muck with a nod of his tam-o'-shantered head.

"As is the case on the final day of play, referees ride with the top five teams." A broad, taunting smile blossomed on the starter's face. "I will be riding with Muck and his crew on their final round."

"That should make for an interesting round," whispered Clawson.

"Maybe for Mac," Verdu observed. "I think it'll be a big pucker factor for Muck and the boys."

"Edgar, here," gestured McTavish, "will be riding with the Dempsey team…"

As the head starter continued with his presentation, the thought of winning the tournament began to settle in, bringing a smile to Dempsey's face.

"What's so funny?"

Dempsey turned to Clawson. The Southerner had noted the other man's expression.

"I was just thinking that we might win this thing."

Clawson smiled. "I was just thinking the same thing."

"So, if there are no questions," McTavish concluded, "best of luck to all the teams, and let's get started."

The room exploded in activity as players moved towards the exits.

As Dempsey and his team turned to leave, they were blocked by Muck, Pfunke, Baxter, and Howe. Dempsey looked Muck in the eye and offered the other man his hand.

"Looks like you're on your way to another win, T.J."

The large man smirked. "You sound surprised."

Dempsey shrugged, lowering his unacknowledged hand. He wasn't going to let the other man get his goat.

"You're not thinking of throwing in the towel, are you?"

"Not likely," Clawson stated.

"That's good to hear," Muck answered. "I'd hate to miss out on beating you guys soundly."

"Don't worry, T.J." Pearsall took a position behind Dempsey. "We'll give you a run for your money." He lowered his voice and flipped his head conspiratorially towards Pfunke. In a stage whisper, he asked: "Are you going to tell him about the dead squirrel on his head, or should I?"

"That's not funny," protested Pfunke. His protest would have carried more weight had Muck and Baxter not laughed.

"We'll see you out there." Muck turned to leave, then turned back to face his competitors. "Not that it will make a difference, but good luck."

"I really don't like those guys," Verdu stated, watching as Muck and the others departed the banquet hall. "It would sure be nice to kick their asses."

"If only so we wouldn't have to see that butt-ugly tuxedo Muck wears." The image of Muck in his green and white tuxedo with the golfing motif caused Pearsall's lip to curl in disgust.

"Maybe he'd wear it anyway," Dempsey observed. "Hell, that may be the best suit he owns."

"I hope you're wrong," Pearsall said.

"There's only one way to find out," observed Clawson.

The four men fell silent. Around them, the other players were slowly making their way from the large room.

McTavish appeared beside them. "You gentlemen might want to get to your tee."

"We're the last out on the North," Dempsey answered.

McTavish nodded.

"Well, then, don't be late. And best of luck to you." The Scot graced each man with a smile.

"Thanks," Dempsey said.

"Don't thank me, lads," he smiled. "Just win."

The Scotsman strode from the room, head high and proud.

"You heard the man," Pearsall said. "Let's go win a golf tournament."

* * * * *

By the time they reached the turn, Dempsey and the others had closed the gap with Muck, or so they hoped. If Muck and the others were playing par golf, they had closed, and possibly passed, their rivals. On the other hand, if Muck, Pfunke, Baxter, and Howe were on a roll, then Dempsey and his pals were, at best, treading water.

And Edgar was no help at all.

The aged referee carried a large walkie-talkie with him, ostensibly to maintain contact with the other officials, but he seemed loath to use the device unless there was some ruling he might need a second opinion on. It was their bad luck that Edgar had committed the USGA rules to memory. For all the use the walkie-talkie received, it might just as well have been a rock.

Pearsall and Verdu had taken the lead on subtle efforts to get Edgar to check in with McTavish and find out how Muck was doing. The referee, however, seemed impervious to subtlety. It wasn't until Clawson asked the man outright to contact McTavish that the definitive answer was forthcoming.

"No status communications are allowed," the man answered. "McTavish wants you to play your best, not just as good as you need to win."

"And what," Verdu challenged, "if our best isn't good enough?"

"Then it won't matter," the old man answered, smiling.

And the round continued.

The tenth, a straight par four, gave them no problems. In fact, they were able to pick up a stroke.

The eleventh, a par three where the tee and the green were separated by a rocky valley, notorious with club members for attracting and concealing balls, lived up to its reputation. Pearsall topped his tee shot, sending his ball deep into the scrub of the valley.

The stroke gained was quickly lost.

And then regained.

Then lost again.

There was Verdu's chip shot from beyond the greenside bunker that rolled to within a foot of the pin. And Dempsey's thirty-foot putt on thirteen, turning and twisting like a snake with gas, that ultimately found the hole.

There was Pearsall's drive of a lifetime on fifteen, a sweet, gentle draw that followed the slight dogleg left like a hawk following a warm trail. The drive set him up for a birdie putt, just one of the better holes of the day.

But the fine, made-for-television shots that lifted the team's spirits were counterbalanced by the missed putts, sculled bunker shots, chili pepper chip shots, and mind fart drives and second shots.

The back nine was a roller-coaster ride of a round, made all the more exciting, all the bigger a challenge, because they were that much closer to winning. And winning the Van Courtland Glen Annual Golf Tournament had become much more than a trophy, prime parking spaces, the glowing admiration of one's fellow club members, and undisputed bragging rights for a year. Taking the trophy was minor when compared to taking Muck down a notch or two.

As play progressed, under Edgar's watchful and humorless eye, Dempsey, Pearsall, Verdu, and Clawson played with more passion, confident that they not only could win, but would win, in spite of drawing the more demanding North Course for their final round. They were playing better golf than they'd ever played before, either alone or as a foursome. They were 'on', 'in the zone', 'wearing their game faces', and a whole host of other, meaningless euphemisms coined to inarticulately describe the indescribable focus of an athlete playing to win.

Their usual banter trailed off, none of them wanting to distract the other, or wishing to lose focus. The game, for the first time for any of them, was serious. They weren't going to die or lose their families, no matter the outcome, but the outcome had become important to them because, as a team, and as individuals, they had invested their egos in the success of this one round of golf.

Luck and skill had combined to put them in a position to win the tournament. They might have reached that decision late in the game, but their dedication was no less sincere for its tardy arrival.

The humid afternoon went unnoticed as they entered the tee box on eighteen.

"This is it, guys." Clawson peered off down the fairway of the par five. Around a stand of trees in the distance, unseen from the tee, was the eighteenth green, the clubhouse, and the results of the tournament. "We begin our final march to destiny."

Pearsall snorted.

"Pah-leeze," drawled Verdu.

"A bit too thick?" Clawson looked from one to the other of his foursome.

Dempsey nodded, smiling.

Even Edgar allowed himself a pleased sneer.

"However this ends up," Clawson said, looking at his teammates, "it has been a true honor to play with you gentlemen."

"And you," Pearsall echoed.

"You make it sound like we're riding over this hill into the shadow of the Valley of Death..."

"...rode the brave six hundred..."

"...or the misguided four?"

"We've done our best up until now," Dempsey stated. "This final hole, this par five, will tell the tale."

"Gentlemen," interrupted Edgar. "Please."

Each man looked a bit chagrinned, but the importance of the hole was lost on no one.

"Who has honors?"

"Screw honors," Verdu said. "I'm ready to go."

The small, bullish man stepped up, teed his ball, and sent it sailing down the fairway. He was followed in quick succession by Pearsall, Clawson, and Dempsey.

The four were well warmed up by the eighteenth, but what they'd gained in bug-free play, they'd lost to fatigue. Given the sun, the heat, the humidity, and the focus, they were very tired and they struggled as much with that as with the course.

The drives were solid fairway rollers, but Pearsall's second shot was a classic example of tired play; his three wood dug a long divot into the grass that began three inches behind the ball before making contact. The ball only managed a labored sixty yards.

"At least it was straight," observed Verdu, encouragingly.

No other comments were needed. They'd all been there before.

Dempsey's third shot, an easy seventy-yard pitch, was another victim of fatigue.

Instead of a simple eight iron 'bump and run' onto the green, or an equally easy sand wedge floater, he inadvertently grabbed his nine iron, too much club for the distance before him. Before he'd realized his mistake, or Clawson, who'd noticed the club selection but didn't register the potential error in time, Dempsey stepped up, settled, and took his swing.

As bad as it could have been, the mental lapse was offset by his aching knees. He hadn't settled into his stance deeply enough.

Thinking he'd made the right club selection...the sand wedge...Dempsey took a full swing, but instead of the ball sailing over the green, landing some distance beyond the target, he topped the ball, sending a low, bouncing 'screamer' at the pin. Bounding along the fairway took some of the speed off the ball, which meant that the ball came to rest just on the edge of the far side of the green.

"What the...?" Dempsey muttered angrily, watching the ball scurry like a scalded rodent across the green.

"Wrong club," Clawson stated, blotting his neck with his towel.

Dempsey looked disbelievingly at his nine iron. "Damn!"

"At least it was a good miss."

"Yeah," the frustrated golfer nodded, "and it was straight, too."

Clawson laughed.

Once on the green, Dempsey was looking at his long birdie putt. Pearsall and Verdu, struggling to get to the green, had managed to leave themselves very easy par putts. Clawson, ever cool and contained, had left himself a five-foot birdie putt. As the men assessed their lies, McTavish appeared on the edge of the green.

"You've been playing quite a round, I'm told." The stoic Scot, dressed in his tam, jacket, and woolen kilt, should have spontaneously combusted in the late August heat. Instead, he looked as cool as Ben Nevis in January.

"How do you do it, Mac?" Verdu removed his ball cap and wiped his brow with the hem of his already damp shirt. "I'm about ready to drop, and I'm dressed for the weather."

"Dealing with the heat is like golf, Mr. Verdu. Ninety percent of the game is mental," he observed, winking, "and the other ten percent is mental."

"Well," Dempsey said, drying the grip on his putter, "I'm certainly glad you explained that."

"Me, too." Clawson looked around. For the first time he noticed the crowd that was edging the area behind them. The crowd was growing.

"What's this," he asked, indicating the people nearing the green.

"You're the last group to finish," the Scot stated.

"So Muck is..."

"Don't ask," the kilted man admonished. "You know I can't tell you how they did."

"Right."

"On the other hand," the Scot smiled, "they have no idea how you're doing. If it's any consolation," he chuckled, "they're like a group of St. Leonard's girls on Shampoo Day."

Even Edgar was flummoxed by that one.

"They're concerned and apprehensive," McTavish clarified, noting the confusion on everyone's face.

The other men nodded.

Dempsey surveyed the crowd. He'd never had a gallery before and wasn't sure what to think.

"If you want," the Scot offered, "I can ask them to leave."

They considered the people down by the green, and those lining the railing of the veranda. All the tournament participants appeared to be there, along with more than a few on-lookers.

Dempsey could feel the pressure building. Maybe we should have McTavish clear the course, he thought, and then he spotted Muck, at the front of the railing, flanked by his teammates, a wicked smile contorting his face. He tipped his ball cap to the men on the green, a gesture that no one mistook for a salute of good sportsmanship.

"Prick," Pearsall muttered, smiling and acknowledging Muck with a wave.

"Leave the crowd, Mac." Dempsey looked to his teammates, each nodding their agreement in turn.

As Dempsey approached his putt, the crowd fell quiet and still. It was always difficult to fathom how a game played outdoors, attended by so many people, on such a spacious area like a green, could become so quiet.

Odd, he thought, but I don't feel any pressure to make the putt. He chanced a quick look at his friends. Their faces were calm, passive. He got the feeling that if he made the putt, they'd be ecstatic, but if he didn't make the putt, well, that would be okay, too. It was a game, after all, and other than the odd nature of this particular tournament, it had been no different than years past.

Except for Arnie P.

Dempsey stepped away from his ball, looking again at the tightly cut grass lying between his ball and the cup.

He missed his dog. With all the help he'd provided during the tournament, the little guy deserved to be here, to be involved in how it ended.

"Mr. Dempsey?" Edgar had moved to within three feet of the man lining up his putt. "You're away."

It was a gentle reminder that play must continue.

"Travis?" Pearsall waved the referee away. "You okay?"

"I was just thinking how nice it would be if Arnie P. was here."

The tall man nodded. "I miss him, too. More than I thought I would." He smiled. "Certainly more than is normal, or possibly healthy, for a non-pet owner."

"It would be nice to have him here, though."

"Yeah," Pearsall agreed, nodding, "but in fairness to Arnie P., we never once lost a ball on the green, so the little guy would be useless to us now."

Dempsey smiled.

"Listen, take your time and line this putt up. Once this tourney's over, we'll take some time and go looking for the little fella. Our caseload's light and we have some time coming. Oh, and we own the practice so we can do what we want, remember?"

"They've had all sorts of searches. They didn't find any of the dogs."

"They weren't motivated."

"Motivated?"

"They didn't love Arnie P. like we do. We'll find him. Hell, the little shit's probably having the time of his life. Getting laid. Eating fresh woodchuck. Not even giving us a second thought."

Dempsey laughed. "I got ya."

"Then sink this putt and let's go."

Pearsall stepped to the side of the green as Dempsey rose and settled in for his birdie putt. His head directly over the ball, he looked from the ball to the hole, then back to the ball. The face of the putter rested lightly on the grass behind the ball.

It was a thirty-foot putt that went right to left, but there was a slight rise in the first ten feet. Dempsey needed to hit the ball hard enough to get the ball up the rise and to the hole, with enough give in the direction so that the cant of the green would pull the ball slightly to the left so the ball would fall into cup at the end of the arc. Too soft a putt and the ball would die before the cup. Too hard and the ball, regardless of the slope, would speed past the cup. Too far to the right and the ball would overshoot the hole, not enough to the right and the slope would drag the ball left before the hole.

All the variables registered instantly in Dempsey's mind, and he did what all golfers do; he lined up the shot the best he could…and then said a silent prayer.

The club head came away from the ball, then swung forward and through the ball, the 'click' of the club hitting the ball sounding like a gunshot in the hush of the crowd.

The ball rolled up the mild incline, losing a fraction of speed as it crested the rise. The round, white orb rolled with a stately grace, gravity pulling it gradually from right to left. From one vantage point it looked as though the ball would stop well short of the hole. From another perspective, it looked to have too much 'oomph', doomed to overshoot the target. From Dempsey's perspective, he'd done the best job he could.

On a long putt, golfers never truly know how well they've done until the ball stops rolling. They never know, but they have their suspicions.

Dempsey suspected that he'd hit his ball just right.

The closer the ball rolled toward the hole, the louder the gallery became, as though the ball were a sliding volume control. Heads moved slowly, following the progress of the putt.

Three feet from the cup, the ball slowed and, more importantly, took a noticeable hop. Whether it hit a small bit of leaf or twig, or a tiny clump of dirt nestled in the short grass, the ball became airborne for a fraction of a second. The crowd took in an audible, collective breath.

Dempsey stared in wonder. It was the small things that made golf such a challenge, and a little piece of dirt that forced a ball a fraction of an inch off its path could be the difference between an inspired putt and a misread.

Whatever the ball had hit, however, was no match for the ball or the strength of Dempsey's will.

The ball settled quickly and continued its course, edging slightly left...and dropped from view as it fell into the cup.

The crowd erupted in wild cheering as a red-faced Dempsey strode across the green and pulled his ball from the cup.

"Great putt, Travis." Verdu patted his friend on the back as he stepped up to his ball marker. "Nice birdie."

Verdu, laying four, had a ten-foot putt to make par. Almost without thinking, the short, bullish man placed his ball, pocketed his marker, gave the ground between the ball and cup a cursory examination, and then putted.

The ball rolled straight into the cup.

Again, the crowd cheered.

"I wish you'd take just a little more time on your reads," Pearsall stated. "Watching you putt is like watching a forty yard dash."

Verdu smiled, tipping his hat playfully to the gallery. "I'd just screw it up if I thought about it."

Pearsall stepped past the smaller man and placed his ball above his marker.

"Put this one away, big guy." Verdu pocketed his ball and went to stand next to Dempsey.

Pearsall, also laying four, had a shorter par putt than Verdu. It was a straight five-foot putt, but his ball was above the hole with a slight downward slope. He had to hit the ball hard enough to get it going and get it to the hole; the slope wasn't severe enough to pull the ball along once it started moving. Unfortunately, the downward slope was severe enough to increase the speed of the ball in its five-foot run. If Pearsall hit it too soft, the ball might not make the cup; too hard and the ball could speed by the cup or, more embarrassingly, hit the far lip of the hole and bounce out of the cup.

In many ways Pearsall's putt was more difficult than Dempsey's. The most significant difference was that no one had expected Dempsey to sink his long putt. Everyone expected Pearsall to sink his.

Pearsall examined the five feet of green between his ball and the cup. He stooped next to ball, behind his ball, behind the cup, and paced around both to get a feel for the slope.

The crowd was quiet, but growing restless.

The tall man in the bright Hawaiian shirt took a crouched stance behind the ball. He seemed to shrink to half his size as he hunkered down for his putt. He took one last look at the cup, then focused his attention on the ball.

He took a breath and held it.

The putter came back less than two inches from the ball, and then moved smoothly to the ball.

The ball rolled straight towards the cup. It was obvious to everyone that the ball was accelerating.

Pearsall muttered invective under his breath.

The ball hit the cup just to the left of dead center. It leaned into the cup, but rolled around the upper edge, following the curve of the hole. At any point along its path, the ball could have popped out of the cup and rolled away.

But it didn't.

After rolling completely around the cup's lip, gravity pulled the ball into the cup.

The crowd, holding its breath, exploded into cheers and applause when the ball disappeared from sight.

"A victory lap," smiled Clawson. "Cocky, but well executed."

"These people need some excitement in their lives," countered Pearsall, waving appreciatively to the crowd. "Your putt's as close to a gimme as they get."

Clawson laughed, patting Pearsall on the shoulder.

The Southerner placed his ball within two feet of the cup. Laying three, he was looking at every golfer's dream...a 'gimme' birdie putt. A simple, easy stroke of the putter and it would all be over.

Clawson looked at his putt, carefully clearing a bit of dirt from the ball's path.

He settled in behind the ball and gave the ball a light tap with his putter.

The ball rolled slightly right of the hole, catching the right lip of the cup. Like Pearsall's putt, the ball began skirting the upper edge of the cup. Unlike Pearsall's putt, the ball jumped the lip and rolled to the left of the cup, coming to rest six inches from the hole.

The moan of disappointment from the gallery was deafening.

Clawson didn't look up or in any way acknowledge the presence of anyone else in the area.

He stepped up to the ball, aligned his putter, and sank his six-inch putt.

"Bad luck, Rex." Dempsey stepped forward and offered his hand. They were quickly joined by Pearsall and Verdu.

"That may have cost us," Clawson admitted. "I'm sorry."

"Don't worry, Rex," Verdu offered. "We've been playing for three months. There were plenty of other shots we could have made and didn't."

"Yeah," Pearsall agreed. "We didn't win or lose based on that putt."

Dempsey laughed. "I agree," he said, "it just happens to be the most publicly witnessed missed putt."

Clawson smiled.

And then they all became aware of the crowd. Their fellow players were crowding in around them, offering congratulations. Those who couldn't make it to the last four golfers were applauding the effort.

McTavish appeared in the midst of the throng.

"Come along, gentlemen," he said, the sound of his brogue quieting the crowd. "You've got to turn in your card and your thirty minutes are ticking away."

* * * * *

The sun was slipping behind the tall trees on the back of the property, a deep red glow coating the feathery edges of the random clouds floating lazily across the sky.

From the dining room window, Dempsey had a panoramic view of his property, Donna's gardens, the swimming pool where he'd taught his children to swim, and the expanse of tall grass where Arnie P. had first demonstrated his skills as a golf dog. If he squinted his eyes he could almost see the frisky Jack Russell bounding from the tall grass into their neatly trimmed back yard, ears cocked forward, eyes clear and focused, and head tilted to one side, as though hearing a distant, engaging sound.

Dempsey's eyes misted slightly. Since finishing the tournament he'd been doing a lot of thinking.

They'd lost the tournament by one stroke. One stroke! Clawson's birdie putt would have forced a three-hole playoff. There had been no playoff, but that bothered him less than Arnie P.'s absence. He'd been thinking a lot about Arnie P. since getting home, and the more he thought of his missing friend, the more despondent he'd become. And the liquor didn't help his mood improve.

Dempsey had finished a nearly empty bottle of Johnnie Walker Blue, and then started in on a bottle of expensive single malt, a gift from a happy client. After the first three shots of the Blue, he might just as well have been drinking 'kill-me-quick' scotch. It would have tasted the same to him and still kept his mood dark and brooding.

"Will he be all right?"

Donna stood in the kitchen doorway, with Lauren on her right and Cliff on her left. The three of them had been watching Dempsey drink. Lauren had become increasingly concerned.

"He'll be fine, honey." Donna put an arm around each of her children. They had never seen their father in such a funk, and the change was unsettling for them. Donna knew her kids, and knew her husband, and was certain that there would be no lasting damage from the kids seeing their father in such a state. "Your father is just upset with himself."

"It's just a game," Cliff stated.

"It's not the game," Donna said, squeezing her son's shoulder. "It's Arnie P."

At the mention of the dog's name, Cliff teared up. His head rested against his mother's side.

"I miss him," the boy whispered.

"Me, too," parroted Lauren.

"We all do," Donna admitted. "Especially your dad."

"Then why did he get him lost?"

"He didn't mean to," their mother assured them. "It was a plan..."

"...a bad plan..."

"...that didn't turn out the way he'd hoped. It happens sometimes."

"To dad?" The thought of his father being less than perfect was a frightening concept to the eleven-year-old boy. Like a loose tooth, though, it had to be explored, regardless of the pain.

"To everyone," Donna answered. "You can't go through life without making mistakes," she said. "It's how we gain experience. It's how we learn."

"What will dad learn," Lauren wondered.

"To leave Arnie P. at home," offered Cliff.

Donna nodded.

"That maybe wearing glasses isn't the end of the world?" Lauren looked at her mother for validation.

Donna nodded again.

"Your father's like all men," she said. "Growing old is scary."

"Dad's not afraid of anything." Cliff felt a need to step up to his father's defense.

"Your father is a very brave man," Donna said. She had a sudden spark of pride in her son. "But the things we can't control always frighten us."

"Like going blind?"

"Your father isn't going blind." Donna stifled a laugh. "But needing glasses is a sign of aging."

"Just like a reclining hairline," offered Cliff, sagely.

"Yes," smiled Donna, wondering again where children came up with such things, "just like a reclining hairline."

The three of them watched as Dempsey, his back to them, took another swallow of his drink.

"He's been sitting there a long time," Lauren observed.

"He really feels badly about Arnie P. He just has to work it out the best way he knows how."

"But Mom," Lauren began, her voice lowering to near inaudibility, "he shouldn't be drinking. We learned in school that a person can't solve their problems with alcohol. Alcohol makes problems worse."

Donna beamed proudly at her daughter.

"You're quite right, Lauren, and let this be a lesson to you both. Alcohol is neither good nor bad. It's all in how you use it."

Both children listened intently.

"Some people have a high tolerance for liquor, and some have a low tolerance for liquor."

Both children nodded.

"In the case of your father, he has no tolerance for liquor."

The children exchanged confused looks.

Donna sighed. "In three hours your father is going to be as sick as a dog. Tomorrow, he will feel as though he's been beaten with baseball bats, and his head will throb like the bass line of a Coolio rap."

"Doesn't he know?"

"Remember we talked about learning from our mistakes?"

The two children nodded.

"Well, some lessons take time to settle in." Donna smiled, keeping to herself that she, too, lacked any tolerance for liquor. She was as much of a lightweight as her husband, and her most fervent hope was that her children inherited their parents' liquor intolerance.

They waited for an explanation.

"The last time your father got like this was when we got married."

"Dad was upset?" Cliff struggled to understand.

"No, dorkhead," his big sister chided. "He was happy."

"We both were. It was a very special day, and a great party, and every one had a wonderful time. Caught up in the spirit of the occasion, your father forgot that he should never drink too much. That night," she said, her mind harkening back to her wedding night, "he was worse than useless."

"Useless?" Cliff's eyes pleaded for some explanation.

Donna reddened, remembering who her audience was. "He was just very sick," she hurried to say. "The point is not to worry. Your father almost never gets like this. And on those very rare occasions when he does, it's better to let him go."

"So he'll gain experience," Lauren stated, awareness dawning.

"And so he won't end up being useless to you," added Cliff, nodding his understanding.

She sent the children to the den, then took a seat next to her husband at the dining room table.

"So, I was useless to you on our wedding night?"

"You heard?"

"I'm drunk," he said, taking his wife's hand and giving it a squeeze, "not dead."

"You'll wish you were in a few hours," Donna stated, "not to mention how you're going to feel tomorrow night at the Gala."

Dempsey nodded.

"As to our wedding night, you've more than made up for it."

"Thanks." He looked at the half filled glass of scotch on the table in front of him. "But I don't think I can be jollied out of this."

"I'm not trying to cheer you up, darling." She leaned over and kissed his hand. "I know only too well how doggedly you embrace your self-flagellation when you punish yourself. I also know, as do you, that what happened with Arnie P. was your fault, but there was no malicious intent. It was an accident. It could have happened to anyone…and it has…but the fact that it happened to you just makes it worse."

He looked at his wife and was reminded again why he loved her so.

"You argue a good case," he slurred. "You should have been a lawyer."

"There is no need to be insulting about this," she joked.

He allowed himself a smile.

"Arnie P. will come back or he won't," she continued. "My money is on him coming back."

"And if he doesn't?"

Donna shrugged. "Your children will never forgive you, you'll become so obsessed with it that your practice will suffer, you'll lose all your clients, Mitch will take the firm from you, and I'll leave you for a man with a dozen housebound cats."

Dempsey stared at his wife in disbelief.

"You'd leave me for a cat guy?"

"You are so drunk," she laughed.

"Cats?" He reached for the glass of scotch. Donna gently took his wrist.

"Let me get you some coffee," she offered. "You may yet manage to get some sleep tonight and spare yourself unnecessary pain."

He handed her the glass. "You're probably right," he acknowledged.

She smiled warmly.

"You think the kids understand?"

"What they can," she answered, taking the glass and the bottle of scotch from the table. She walked towards the kitchen.

"You really think he'll come back?"

Donna stopped and looked at her husband. She couldn't remember ever seeing him so upset. It was both endearing and a little unsettling. How fragile we are, she thought. How little it takes to tilt our worlds from their normal, steady orbits.

She mustered the best smile she could.

"If I didn't," she stated, "I'd have gotten a glass and joined you."

THE GALA

The Fall's Eve Gala, the formal dinner dance at the end of summer, was the single biggest event at the club. No effort was spared to ensure that the grounds were at their pristine best, and every effort was made to clearly demonstrate to the club's membership that they were getting good value for their exorbitant dues. It was a low pressure, high fashion party, and the last big blowout of the summer.

The day of the gala always began early. The housekeeping staff, augmented by twenty people from a local cleaning company, arrived at dawn to clean, sweep, dust, and polish every inch of the massive clubhouse. Particular attention was paid to the entry and the banquet hall.

The club's entry hall was a wide, plush corridor, and served as the formal entrance for the gala. Waiters greeted arriving guests with glasses of champagne and smiles. Lining both sides of the entry hall were the photos, plaques, trophies, and general memorabilia associated with the Van Courtland Glen Country Club since its inception. Running the gauntlet of the past triumphs of the club was a traditional part of the event, and the objects contained in the cases, along with the cases themselves, were cleaned and polished to a high gloss.

The banquet hall received special scrutiny and was gone over with a fine-toothed comb before the first table was brought in for placement. The huge windows of the banquet hall, overlooking the flagstone veranda that, in turn, overlooked the first fairway of the North Course all the way to the distant green, were meticulously cleaned to provide the gala's attendees an unobstructed view of the evening's capping event, a twenty minute fireworks display.

By midmorning the building was cleaned from top to bottom, and the task of setting up the banquet hall for nearly three hundred guests, as well as a twelve-piece band, began in earnest. The job of setting up thirty tables large enough to seat ten was a major undertaking, all of which had to be done before the linens and place settings could be set.

While the hall was being set up, the kitchen staff was hard at work prepping the evening's meal. All the ingredients for all phases of the meal, brought fresh that morning, were carefully cleaned, trimmed, topped, tailed, or peeled.

The kitchen was a singularly large, rectangular work area and readily allowed the thirty people making up the kitchen staff to move easily about the kitchen without getting in each other's way. The key to the successful running of the kitchen was in always keeping the broad center aisle clear. The center aisle ran in a straight line from the back door of the kitchen to the swinging service doors into the banquet hall. There were doors on one side of the kitchen for servicing the bar and the two other, smaller dining rooms, but the kitchen had been designed to feed large numbers of guests. In order to do that successfully, the center of the kitchen remained clear at all times.

While the clubhouse staff busily prepared for the evening festivities, the grounds crews were hard at work on the courses and around the clubhouse.

On the day of the Fall's Eve Gala, no golf was played at the Van Courtland Glen Country Club. There was too much to be done.

Long before the last of the late summer's dew had been wicked from the grass, crews were busy trimming the greens and fairways. Trees along the fairways and cart paths were tended, and underbrush cleared. Even the distance markers in the fairways and on the paths were given a fresh coat of paint, as were the various out buildings adjacent to, and within sight of, the clubhouse. Every effort was made to give the appearance of a golf course captured on film, and showcased in Golfer's World Magazine. This was particularly true of the number one hole of the North Course.

The first tee was adjacent to the eighteenth green and stood proudly beneath the large, gently curving veranda of the clubhouse. From the veranda a member could as easily watch a round finish as begin, but where the eighteenth turned into the clubhouse, the par four number one was a straight, gently sloping, deceptively challenging four hundred and sixty-five yards. It was not unusual to find members enjoying a drink on the veranda while following a foursome from tee to green.

Because of the special place the number one North held for the membership, and because it was the only fairway clearly visible from the banquet hall, special attention was given to cleaning and grooming the hole. So exacting was the care that a new stick and flag were installed on the green, and understanding that a normal sized flag would be difficult to see from the clubhouse, a specially designed oversized flag was used. If anyone thought such an accommodation was particularly stupid or wasteful, they kept it to themselves.

As an added treat for the members, not to mention the club's neighbors, Van Courtland Glen ended their gala with a traditional fireworks display, the perfect coda to a summer of fun, sport, and competition.

The club contracted with the region's premiere pyrotechnic specialists, The Landino Brothers, for its fireworks. The Landino Brothers were the company of choice for pyrotechnics from Baltimore to Beaufort, no small feat given the competition, but the company founder, at the turn of the century, had bested their competition through competitive pricing and sheer doggedness. Their creativity with all things explosive also lent greatly to their demand, for the Landino's were always coming up with new, exciting, and mostly legal ways to amaze their audiences.

For this particular event the Landino Brothers promised something special, a unique, never-before-seen, one-of-a-kind firework made just for Van Courtland Glen for the party. What the Landino Brothers hadn't shared with the board was that the unique firework was never-before-seen and one-of-a-kind because it had never been tried before. The Landino Brothers hired creative people to construct new and amazing missiles and clusters, but they didn't waste time or money on testing. If they could get a rocket off the ground and have it explode in the air, and there were no injuries, why worry about testing? There seemed to be no point to it, given that their business was making loud, brilliant bombs, and a louder, brighter explosion was viewed as a plus by their audiences.

The firework's staging area was just to the side of the second tee on the North Course. This spot was open and accessible, but was shielded from view of the clubhouse and veranda by a thicket of dense trees and bushes. From the clubhouse it would seem as though the fireworks were appearing, fully formed, in the night sky.

The two men from Landino Brothers began setting up late in the morning. They'd set up the six rows of ten, thick metal tubes, each serving as a mortar barrel directing projectiles skyward. They were held in place by a wooden frame and anchored to the ground with sandbags.

A safe distance away, resting on two sawhorses, was a large, rectangular control panel with row after row of labeled switches. Once the ignition charges were wired into the panel, and then the panel was connected to the car battery under the panel, the entire display could be controlled from that one spot. Unfortunately, the ground was not level, so the sawhorses wobbled slightly. The two men were less concerned about the stability of the panel than they were about the mystery firework.

Off to one side, away from the other firework tubes, sat a simple, single, thick tube. It was twice as long as the other tubes and had a wider bore. It was held upright by a stack of sandbags three deep and three feet high. The bags came nearly to the top of the tube. Half as many bags would have held the tube in place, but the bulk of the bags were there to contain the explosion, if the rocket couldn't make it out of the tube.

The special firework for that night had been brought to the staging area in a bright red cooler, packed in dry ice. The cooler sat next to the buttressed firing tube. Streams of vapor poured from the holes drilled along the top and sides of the cooler. It looked as though it might explode at any moment. In truth, the technicians with Landino's weren't at all certain that the firework wouldn't explode. They just hoped that the dry ice would buy them a little time.

The two men setting up the display moved in well-practiced motions, confident in what they were about. Occasionally, one or other of the men would sneak a peek at the misting cooler and shake his head in wonder.

* * * * *

The driving ranges were closed. All of the range balls had been collected, cleaned, and put into plastic buckets by each of the ball machines. A dozen such buckets, filled with sparkling white golf balls, sat beside the wonky ball machine. The machine itself was in the process of getting one last touch of paint, a dark green designed to give the large, boxy metal machine the appearance of something natural, as though color alone could overcome the alien form of the box. The machine chunked and warbled steadily, as though the stroke of the paintbrush was bringing it pleasure. The worker ignored the noises made by the machine, his attention focused on remaining in place for as long as possible.

Leigh Wolfe had stolen a grounds crew coverall, blending in easily with the pre-gala activity. Since there was so much to do and so many new faces around, no one stopped to wonder about the man whose entire day was spent working on the one ball machine. Besides, it looked as though the guy was trying to fix it, what with tools and wires laid out all around the machine.

Wolfe knew little about the machine's history. Only what Josh had told him. Had he known nothing, he wouldn't have cared. He was there strictly to disrupt the gala, and the wonky ball machine, with the way it randomly fired balls off into space, was just the inspiration he'd hoped for.

The ball machine was thirty feet away from the large, screened double doors of the kitchen. He'd observed the vast expanse of the kitchen's interior when an early delivery was made, and learned that at the far end of the kitchen were the doors to the banquet hall.

The plan was simple: loosen the bolts holding the machine in place, reorient the ball chute upwards so that the balls would be fired in a more or less straight trajectory, turn the machine to face the kitchen doors, and then short the system for continuous fire.

Once turned on, the fusillade of range balls would jet through the kitchen into the banquet hall, totally disrupting the food preparation and the awards event. It wasn't perfect, Wolfe knew, but it would do. And it would achieve his goal of humbling UFLACADAC while once more demonstrating the continued value and existence of ARF.

Small steps, he reminded himself, finishing the last spot of paint.

The sun was lowering in the cloudless sky. It would be an otherwise beautiful evening for a dinner dance.

Wolfe, for the twelfth time, ran over the steps in his mind. All was in order, he thought, turning to see the guests arriving in the distant parking lot.

They were a splendid sight, he had to admit, decked out in their formal wear and jewelry. All, he thought, except that one guy. Wolfe squinted to get a better look at the man wearing what looked like a white tuxedo that had been on the receiving end of a haphazard green paint spill. It was only when the couple came closer that Wolfe could see what had first appeared as random stains were actually patterns. Golf patterns.

Why on earth, he thought…

"Hey, you!"

Wolfe turned from the arriving guests and faced a man clad in a similar coverall.

"Yes?"

"Finish up, will ya. We're supposed to be gone when the guests arrive."

"Will do," Wolfe answered. "Just have to clean up my tools."

"Make it fast!"

Wolfe went through the motions of cleaning his work area until the man disappeared around the corner of the building.

He needed a little more time, but he couldn't risk being seen again without causing suspicion.

A group of bushes off to his right offered him cover. He'd hide there until dark. In the meantime, he could watch the parade of arriving guests.

He wondered, as he moved, if he'd see another tuxedo as striking as the earlier one?

* * * * *

Julia Muck was radiant in her formal satin gown of oyster white. In truth, the tall, slender brunette could wear baggy pants and a sweatshirt and she would be no less striking in her appearance. She was a classic beauty, with high cheekbones, full lips, chocolate brown eyes, and a creamy complexion that seemed never to have been touched by the ravages of the sun or time. She had long ago grown accustomed to heads turning as she passed. It was not an ego thing...it had never been about her ego...just an understanding that her looks drew attention wherever she went. She was comfortable with who she was but, on this particular evening, not completely comfortable with the man she was with.

Striding next to her in that ridiculous, horrendous tuxedo was her husband.

"Did you have to wear that thing," she asked, the smile never leaving her face.

"What," he questioned, "the Victory Tux? Of course I had to wear it. It's tradition, just like me winning the cup. You can't have one without the other."

"Isn't it enough that you've won?"

"That's never enough," he responded, taking particular pride in seeing some of his competitors look away at his approach. They may envy me, or hate me, he thought, but they'll never best me. Never!

He was on top of the world. And it would only get better when the trophy was again placed in his hands and the audience, because it was required and the people were too polite to do otherwise, applauded his accomplishment, an accomplishment they all hoped for, but that continually eluded them. Only he knew how to win the cup, and they had to admire him for that.

Julia had also noticed the turned heads...she'd even noticed one of the ground's crew taking in her husband's tux from over by the ball machine...and was reminded anew of the questions she'd begun to ask herself about her husband and her life.

For years it had been fine that T.J. was the leader of their family, the one whose tone and demeanor defined the Mucks. That had been fine because what the outside world thought or assumed was of little consequence to her. What mattered was what happened inside the family, between the two of them, and that, whatever anyone might think, she and T.J. were equals, and that he cared for her.

At least, that's what she'd thought.

There were little things over the years...the random, unkind word, the forgetting of a birthday, or four, the rudeness to friends...all of which could be explained away, as long as each occurrence were taken in isolation. That was getting harder for her to do. Some of it was new, like losing Cali because his ego had gotten the better of him. Some of it was just her eyes opening a little wider.

And what angered her this particular evening was that damned Victory Tux. He'd had it for years, wearing it every year for the gala, so it wasn't like this was something new. No, she'd known he'd wear the damned, ugly tux with the golf images, and that was the thorn in her side, because she had, for the last five years, asked him not to wear it. The first couple of times it was a novelty, a clever joke that all could enjoy. But the joke had worn thin, ceased to be funny, and finally turned sour, no longer a joke. The Victory Tux represented her husband's dominance over the other club members, like one dog humping another, a message that was lost on no one. It had become an embarrassment for her. The fact that he couldn't see that, or didn't care, and missed the fact that the tux was now symbolic of so much more than he imagined, spoke volumes to her.

She smiled inwardly. To a stranger, the thought of leaving her husband over a suit of clothes was ludicrous, but wasn't that always the way it happened? The volume of hurts, transgressions, insults, and slights was so large, so vast, and covered so much ground over the course of time, that there was too much to grasp. It finally came down to something so small, such a seemingly trivial event that triggered a breakup, that it always appeared to the outside observer that the precipitating event was such a petty thing. It was the final straw, or the tip of the iceberg. Whatever it was, the event itself rarely did justice to all that preceded it.

And all she could see of the iceberg now was the tuxedo.

"I think there will be fireworks tonight."

Julia looked wonderingly at her husband.

"I was just thinking that myself."

* * * * *

Members mixed gaily on the expansive veranda. The cocktail hour that preceded the dinner offered members a chance to meet, to reminisce about the tournament, and to admire one another's finery.

The Dempseys arrived late and were working their way through the throng of members when Verdu's wife, Veronica, spotted the couple and waved.

"The gang's all here," beamed Vince, wearing a new black tuxedo that made him look charmingly like an Emperor Penguin on steroids. His wife stood next to him. She was as tall as her husband, but seemed petite standing next to him. Still, Veronica Verdu radiated charm and strength, and her friends knew how tough a woman she could be. She was either a loyal friend for life or life-long enemy, but she left that decision up to the other person's behavior.

For the Gala she'd worn a simple black gown with a string of pearls that drew the eye like a magnet.

"Those are beautiful pearls," Donna Dempsey remarked, embracing the other woman. "New?"

Veronica nodded. "A special gift for my performance this year."

"You don't play in the annual tournament," observed Dempsey.

"Not everything is golf, Travis." Veronica winked lasciviously and nudged her husband, who blushed like a teenager at his first sock-hop.

Donna Dempsey laughed out loud. She was dressed simply in a form fitting blue dress that complemented her blonde hair, made her eyes sparkle, and showcased her toned physique.

"I see Ronnie's told you about the pearls."

A tall, striking woman entered their small circle with drinks in hand. She handed one to Veronica, and then stepped into Donna's friendly embrace.

Nancy Pearsall carried herself like a high-priced fashion model, an image that was reinforced by her light brown complexion, fine cheekbones, arresting brown eyes, and jet-black, shoulder length hair. To those who didn't know her she appeared to be all but unapproachable and cold. In truth, she was a warm, loving wife and mother with a cutting sense of humor who just happened to be neck-snapping gorgeous.

"You went ahead and wore the dress, I see." Donna Dempsey hugged the black woman, referring to what she was wearing. "It looks wonderful."

The dress in question was just this side of a black body sock with a turtleneck, and would have looked sad or ridiculous on anyone without Nancy's figure. With her long neck and narrow hips, the woman looked regal.

"Did I miss anything?" Mitch Pearsall appeared with two more drinks. He handed one drink to Vince. "Sorry," he said, indicating the drinks, "but I didn't see you arrive."

"Not a problem," Dempsey assured his friend. He was still a bit hungover from his guilt-driven binge of the night before, and the thought of liquor knotted his stomach. "Besides, if I get liquored up I don't know that I could keep my hands off your wife."

"She does look hot," Pearsall agreed, nodding his head approvingly while he licked his lips in a crude, suggestive way. "My wife and I may need to slip out to the car for a quick slap-and-tickle during dinner."

"Only if it's some other wife you're talking about."

"If you insist," Pearsall answered, shrugging.

"You skinny women piss me off," sputtered Veronica, playfully.

"Judging by those pearls," Nancy countered, "it seems you have quite enough man on your hands."

"And knees," the shorter woman stated, again turning her husband red.

"Why, Vince," teased Pearsall, "I don't recall your wife being so randy."

Nancy winked at her husband and squeezed his thigh. "Pearls will do that to a woman, honey."

"I've got some in the car," Pearsall teased.

"Then run and get them."

Pearsall smiled warmly, leaning over and giving his wife a gentle kiss on the cheek.

"When we slip out later."

The tall attorney looked every inch the dignitary in his tuxedo, but he was never far from his passion for Hawaiian shirts. He would never get away with wearing one of his colorful prints with the tuxedo, but a close inspection of his variegated bowtie and cummerbund revealed a number of hibiscus and parrots. He knew fashion, but he was always true to himself.

"Has anyone seen Rex?" Dempsey, returning with two club sodas, posed the question to his golf buddies.

Verdu shook his head.

"I haven't seen or heard from him," Pearsall admitted. "You don't suppose he'd take a pass on the Gala, do you?"

"Not likely," Verdu stated. "He'll show, if for no other reason than to catch Muck's speech."

The others nodded, each wondering just how much worse Muck could be this year. The man seemed incapable of graciousness, kindness, or humility at the best of times.

"You know," Pearsall began, "regardless of what Muck does or doesn't do, we had a hell of a play this year. And we should toast our missing member."

They all raised their glasses.

"To Arnie P."

"To Arnie P.," they all echoed.

Melodic chimes signaled the start of dinner.

* * * * *

As the club members moved from the veranda into the banquet hall, the last rays of sun filtered through the treetops. The sky was clear and the wind was calm, a perfect night for dinner, dancing, and fireworks.

As the diners found their seats, waiters moved from table to table, pouring wine. At the front of the room, next to the podium, were three trophies. Most members would never win one of those trophies, but that understanding would never keep them from hoping, or from playing in the next tournament, or the one after that. They might delude themselves by suggesting that it was just a matter of time, or luck, or both. In their hearts, however, they knew the truth; they played because they loved the game. They loved the camaraderie of the game, the challenge, and the small, intangible rewards of a long drive, a tough birdie putt that rolls like it has eyes, or a flop eagle from fifty yards off the green. Such moments were the core of the game. Muck would be quick to point out that such thinking was all they had, especially since they couldn't win. How else would losers think, he'd argue. But being on top of the hill wasn't always a good thing, and being at the bottom, looking up, wasn't always bad.

*   *   *   *   *

Were Arnie P. able to craft such abstract thoughts for purposes of self- examination, the spirited Jack Russell might well have settled for a meal of raw squirrel and a quick coupling with the poodle bitch that had gone into heat the day before. But such thoughts were beyond Arnie P., just as they were beyond the other occupants of the phosphorescent caves, their attention focused on the Jack Russell terrier making his way slowly, cautiously up the large mound of golf balls.

Arnie P. had spent days tracking his master's scent. He'd taken breaks for food and sleep, but even then it had been a Herculean effort. He was covered in glowing mold dust, smelly, and hungry...he fit right in with the rest of the pack. In spite of all that, he'd never wavered or lost sight of his mission. Somewhere, close to the top of the pile, was his master's golf ball. The miasma of odors and scents on the balls, and just generally in the air, made singling out one unique scent that much more difficult, but it was there, and it was getting stronger the nearer he moved towards the top.

His actions had drawn quite a crowd, both below and on the ledge above. All other activities, it seemed, were forgotten or ignored in favor of watching one of their own pursue some unknown challenge. Only one dog seemed troubled by what he was watching. He, too, was unsure what he was seeing, just as he was unsure what he should do about it.

Caligula would occasionally look to his pregnant mate and whimper his confusion. Snowball's responses swung from ignoring his entreaties to licking his ear affectionately.

At the top of the mound Arnie P's attention was galvanized by a sharp, distinctive scent. In a field of indistinguishable white his senses singled out one ball.

Carefully, slowly, he inched forward, sniffing at the ball. It was wedged between a number of others, and the removal of the one ball would mean a small avalanche. He would have to be quick and decisive, not an easy feat given his tenuous footing. All his attention focused forward.

Sensing a change in the Jack Russell, the other dogs in the cave became still and silent. Only Caligula seemed troubled. He inched closer to the ledge overhanging the golf ball mountain. He sat three feet above the small dog.

Arnie P. shot forward, his snout cutting into the golf balls, sending a small cascade of balls down the pile. His jaws grabbed the ball, but his sudden motion shifted his balance and caused a small shift in the balls under him. He began a slow slide down the side of the mound.

Seeing the small dog with the ball in his mouth was too much for Cali. The Doberman stepped off the ledge onto the shifting mound of balls. The Doberman's weight, unlike the lighter Jack Russell, caused a major and immediate change.

Golf balls tumbled from every side of the pile, and the mound collapsed on itself. Golf balls sprayed in every direction, shooting through the crevice leading into the larger cavern.

As they had been doing for weeks, the dogs began chasing the balls, causing pandemonium throughout the cavern.

The Jack Russell, with his master's ball in his mouth, went unnoticed as he weaved his way through the other dogs, and then out the cave entrance into the night.

His departure was unnoticed by all save the alpha male.

Caligula thundered through the cavern in hot pursuit, his howl echoing into every corner of the den. The other dogs, called by their leader, joined the chase and their voices rang out in canine harmony.

* * * * *

"Did you hear that?"

The two Landino Brothers workers were sitting in a utility cart. They were half way down the second fairway, relaxing with cigarettes, when the thrum of howling dogs issued from the distance.

"It's dogs howling," one of the men stated.

"A lot of dogs."

"Don't worry. They're miles away."

The less concerned of the two picked up the walkie-talkie sitting on the seat between them. They were to start the fireworks promptly at 9:00, unless they heard differently. He checked his watch. They were still an hour out, even though it was dark enough to go at any time.

Off to the west the sky was just growing dark, but the two men were in near total darkness.

"I don't much like dogs," said the younger of the two men.

"I don't much care," was the other man's response. "We've got bigger things to worry about."

The younger man nodded.

They both looked back towards where the fireworks were set up. In one tube, set apart from the others, was the Big Bang, their description of the new pyrotechnic. Neither of them knew what would happen when they set it off. They just knew they needed to be a safe distance away.

* * * * *

The entrees were being served when Clawson and the Widow Hendricks made their entrance.

Dempsey wasn't sure what he'd expected of the recently widowed woman, but Clawson's description of her had led him to believe that she was, at the very least, the direct descendant of Helen of Troy.

The woman was tall, and blonde, and shapely, and with her hair tastefully pulled into a French braid, she was a striking woman. As the couple approached the table, though, Dempsey noticed a wrinkle on her otherwise flawless forehead, and a mole on her exposed shoulder that seemed to him to be just a tad too large to be completely ignored. As she smiled, he couldn't help but notice that her teeth, while beautifully white, were a smidge uneven.

And then he looked at his friend, at the bounce in his step, the smile on his face, and the arm wrapped loosely, but protectively, around the young woman's waist, and he knew that none of it mattered. There was nothing about the Widow Hendricks' appearance or behavior, or personality that would in any way change Clawson's perception of his date, or her perception of her Southern escort.

"She's beautiful," whispered Donna.

"You think so?"

His wife laughed, patting her husband's arm affectionately. "All women in love are beautiful..."

"...just as all pregnant women glow," added Nancy.

"What's everyone talking about?" Eleanor Wentworth, the wife of Fredericksburg's Chief of Police, looked from one person at the table to the next. A handsome woman in her early sixties, she'd led a sheltered life, and her husband, Farley, liked it that way.

"Don't trouble yourself, El." The Chief patted his wife's hand, giving a disapproving look to the others at the table. "Is this conversation necessary?"

Farley Wentworth was a regal looking gentleman with a full head of silvery hair and a deep voice with an authoritarian tone. As the police chief, he was well respected. On a personal level, most thought him a bit of an ass.

"So, what about Clawson?" Pearsall, ignoring the Chief, felt a need to step up on his friend's behalf.

"He's a stud," Veronica stated, dryly.

"Ronnie," cautioned her husband, smiling.

"Always has been," she continued. She patted her husband's leg. "Don't worry, honey. I'm not leaving you for a younger man."

"Take too long to train a new one?" Donna and Veronica had been friends for years, and the younger woman had early on tumbled to her older friend's sense of humor.

"Absolutely," Veronica laughed, winking.

"Good evening, everyone." Clawson and his date approached the table. "I'm sorry we're late."

"Not a problem, Rex." Dempsey stood, followed by the other men at the table.

Clawson smiled sheepishly, urging his date forward. "I'd like to introduce y'all to my friend, Mrs. Constance Hendricks."

The young woman stepped forward, graciously accepting the greetings offered.

It was an awkward moment. No one dared ask the questions that danced frustratingly close to the tips of their tongues, and it was hard to offer condolences, knowing all that was known.

Sensing their frustrations, Constance Hendricks smiled warmly.

"I know you are all dying to know every detail of my husband's death. In time, those details will come out. Suffice it to say for now, he died with his boots on."

Everyone, a bit disappointed, nodded sympathetically.

"And only his boots on," she added, a mix of pique and pleasure tingeing her voice.

Verdu, sipping his drink, sputtered and wiped his chin.

"You have our sympathies, young lady," Veronica offered, eyeing her husband to make certain he wasn't drowning in his drink. "A most unfortunate occurrence, but he did, after a fashion, make his own bed."

Wentworth, knowledgeable of the details, looked wondering at the others at the table. Every effort had been made to protect the reputation of the Ice Cream King and his widow. In spite of the department's best efforts, however, information seemed to have made its way into the public domain.

"More of a leather futon," corrected Constance.

Clawson laughed as he pulled a chair out for his date.

"I think," Wentworth cautioned, "we should not be discussing this. There is an on-going investigation."

"Investigation?" The lawyers at the table were surprised.

The Police Chief nodded knowingly.

"Hogwash," Constance huffed.

"But Mrs. Hendricks…"

"Chief Wentworth," interrupted Constance, "I am the wronged, bereaved widow. I would be truly upset had he died in his sleep, or while rescuing a small child from the Rappahannock. He didn't, and I'm not. If anything, I'm angry, but I can't even muster much of that right now…"

"…but think of your reputation?"

"My reputation is my business, Chief, just as my husband's was his. He did a tragically poor job of protecting his, and I'm hard pressed to see how it is my role to defend the indefensible."

The widow's face reddened as she spoke, but her gaze was as steady and level as the horizon on a clear, calm day.

Clawson reached out and patted her hand. She immediately took his hand and squeezed it tightly.

"Well done, young lady." Veronica Verdu beamed proudly at the other woman. "I like your style. Why haven't we met before now?"

"I was otherwise engaged."

"You were otherwise married," corrected Rex.

Dempsey looked at his friend. He couldn't remember a time when he'd appeared happier. And it was obvious in how the two looked at each other that there was a depth to their relationship.

"What are you grinning at," whispered Donna.

Dempsey shook his head, knowing that he couldn't put into words what he was feeling.

"At any rate," Constance said, "Rex promised me an exciting evening out."

Nancy Pearsall snorted playfully. "He may have oversold you, honey. The Fall Gala is many things, but the word 'exciting' doesn't come to mind when describing it."

Constance turned to Clawson.

"It won't be exciting?"

The Southerner shrugged, signaling the waiter for wine. "I had to tell you something to get you out of your house."

* * * * *

Going by his sense of smell, and whatever memories were floating around in his small doggie brain, Arnie P. made his way through the woods and rocky outcroppings towards the clubhouse.

The going was difficult in the dark. Even with his ability to see better in the dark than humans, it was still slow going. Luckily for the Jack Russell, his pursuers were no better at seeing in the dark than he, and their sense of smell was impaired by their numbers, since moving in a pack made singling out the scent of one dog difficult.

Even so, they were getting closer.

The woods behind him were coming alive with the sound of twigs snapping and the distinct crunch of dried leaves and detritus crushed beneath quick moving paws.

Arnie P. wasn't that far from where he'd left his master. He could feel it. Lacking a refined concept of time, he had no reason to believe that his master and the others wouldn't be where he'd left them.

The small dog moved quickly forward, golf ball held tightly in his mouth. Through the trees ahead he could see that the darkness lessened. An open space beyond the trees.

He could run faster then, but so could the others.

Breathing heavily around the ball, Arnie P. sprinted for the clearing, the sounds of the other dogs growing louder.

* * * * *

Hiding in the bushes, Wolfe listened carefully for any hint of activity nearby. Nothing close, but those dogs in the distance were a troubling addition to the evening.

He'd become aware of the dogs thirty minutes earlier, but their howls had been far away, possibly even further than he'd suspected, given the way sounds bounced through the hills and woods of the Piedmont. He hadn't thought much of it at first, but when the howls grew louder he remembered what Taffy had told him about the missing dogs. The information had provided the catalyst for his plan, but he'd not really considered the ramifications of a large pack of dogs on the prowl. He was an animal lover, and believed in the rights of animals, but he wasn't an idealistic simpleton when it came to animals. They could be very dangerous, even little Fluffy, the family cat. Especially Fluffy, since no one ever suspected the family cat until they were tumbling down the stairs.

And dogs could be worse. Singly, or in pairs, they were generally harmless, more inclined to chase a ball or catch a Frisbee than rip the throat out of an innocent bystander. In a pack, even a small pack, the mob mentality was not that much different than humans, and it didn't take much to get the feral ball rolling.

You just never know, he thought, certain now that the dogs were much closer. It was still hard to tell from which direction the howls were originating.

Well, he thought, the sooner I get this over with, the sooner I can get out of here.

Leigh Wolfe crawled from behind the bushes, pulling his tool bag behind him.

Noise from the kitchen filtered through the double screen doors out into the darkness. Careful to stay clear of the halo of light spilling from the kitchen, Wolfe moved towards the ball machine.

As though greeting an old friend, the mechanical metal box chugged and thunked twice.

There wasn't much else to do. A few minor adjustments and some careful snips of wires and the machine was ready to go.

Not like the old days, he thought, opening his bag and extracting a wrench, when explosions rang out through the cities, and flames filled the night sky with a cleansing orange glow. No, he conceded, none of that tonight.

But a little, potentially threatening, mayhem was a good start.

A good start, indeed.

* * * * *

"Perhaps," McTavish began, stepping to the podium, "we should get started."

The audience applauded the diminutive kilt-clad man. Many, through hoots and whistles, acknowledged the formal Bonnie Prince Charlie jacket he'd donned, complemented nicely by the plush, white rabbit fur sporran adorning the front of his kilt.

"I see that you've all got your puddin's and trifle, so go on with your eatin' and I'll get on with the festivities."

Polite applause greeted his statement, though it was unclear whether it was the food or the function that had drawn the response.

"As you are all aware, tonight is not just an excuse to tart up and indulge yourselves beyond the bounds of good taste and manners."

The Starter of the Courses had been gently chiding the members for their conspicuous consumption for as long as anyone could remember. The words hadn't changed much over the years, and it never got more personal than a mild dig at the audiences glitzy outfits and copious quantities of food and liquor consumed. Instead of drawing the ire of those present, it was deemed an honor to be chaffed by such a revered icon of the Van Courtland Glen Country Club.

"No," he continued, "tonight is an excuse to tart up, eat and drink too much, *and* recognize this year's winners of the annual Van Courtland Glen Golf Tournament."

Rowdy applause filled the room.

"And while we could, quite easily, waste more time with idle blather and chat about this team or that, let's get on with it."

He reached into his sporran and pulled out a pair of reading glasses.

"Though all the teams played well this year, there are only three trophies."

Everyone knew which team was getting which trophy. It was, after all, a tournament, not the Academy Awards. Even so, while the outcome was known to all present, it was still exciting to hear the winners announced.

"But before I go further, I should acknowledge the club's loss of Mr. Hendricks."

Quiet, respectful applause.

"His team was on line to finish high in the standings this year, but an untimely accident forced the team to forfeit." McTavish folded the piece of paper he'd been reading from and slipped it into his jacket pocket. "If you'll allow me, please raise a glass to the departed Mr. Hendricks and his unfortunate team."

Glasses were raised and honors offered.

"So now we move on." He turned to the table next to the podium.

Resting on the table were the three trophies. The smallest, closest to the podium, was little more than a Jefferson Cup planted atop a miniature Doric column, that rested on a polished block of wood. A narrow brass plaque, affixed to the wooden base, contained the names of the 3rd place winners. At the far end of the table was the 2nd place trophy, a large, gold chalice set upon a block of white marble. A gold plaque on the marble block contained the names of the 2nd place team members. The largest of the three, positioned between the other two trophies, was the cherished, much sought after Van Courtland Glen Cup, which was actually a large silver bowl on a mahogany pedestal. The names of the winners were engraved on the bowl proper, along with the dates of the tournament, and their final score.

The lights focused on the podium reflected off the trophies, but it was the large bowl in the center of the table that drew the most attention.

Taking the small trophy nearest him, McTavish raised the item over his head.

"In third place," he intoned, and called the winners to the front of the room.

* * * * *

The hounds were drawing closer. The two men from Landino Brothers, in the process of double-checking the connections from the firing panel, chanced to turn and face the direction of the ever-nearing howls.

"You think we'll be okay?" The younger of the two men had gone pale in the faint yellow light from their flashlights. "I mean, I've heard stories about the wild dogs in the hills."

"Stop it," the older man warned. "You've lived here all your life, as have I. This is the first year I've ever heard tell of wild dogs in the hills."

"That doesn't make it wrong."

"No, but it sure as shit makes it coincidental," the older man chided. He checked his watch, holding his flashlight up to his wrist, then took the leads from the car battery sitting at his feet and connected the alligator clips to the contacts on the firing panel.

"It's getting near time," he said. "We're hot now."

Once the battery was connected to the board, and the board was connected to the small charges at the bottom of each firing tube, all that remained to do was for the two men to push the buttons on the board, in the scripted sequence, to light up the night sky.

They carefully taped over the button on the far right of the panel, the ignition switch for the big finale.

Earlier, they had gingerly removed the experimental pyrotechnic from the red cooler and, just as carefully, loaded it into its specially reinforced firing tube. The tube, set away from the rest, made both men nervous. The sound of the hounds wasn't lessening that anxiety.

"Let's double check the bundles," the older man said. Truth be known, he wasn't happy about being out in the dark with a new, untested explosive device and what sounded like the entire cast, including stunt doubles, of that Dalmatian movie. Still, the weather was nice, and in another thirty minutes they'd set the show off and be on their way.

Not long now, he reminded himself.

The younger man had begun checking the wires that ran from the tubes to the firing board that rested precariously on its two sawhorses. The ground between the tubes and the board looked like a snake parade in the dark, a massive tangle of wires that appeared darker than the ground around them.

The young man's attention was split between the job he was doing and the howls of the approaching dogs. As he tried to bundle wires together, the panel rocked precariously on its perch.

"Careful," hissed the other man. "You want to blow us up?"

"Sorry."

The two men were busy putting the finishing touches on their preparations when a singular noise intruded on the young man's thoughts.

"You hear that?"

"Would you stop?"

"No," he insisted. "Really."

"Really, what? What was I supposed to hear?"

"It sounded like panting."

"Panting?"

"Yeah, like some animal panting."

The howling died briefly. In its place could be heard what sounded like rhythmic, wheezy breathing.

"Sounds like panting," said the older man.

"See?"

"And it's coming this way."

Both men turned in the direction of the noise. They were looking down the second fairway of the North Course, and they could just make out a fast moving greenish glow racing towards them.

"What is that?" The young man's voice betrayed his fear.

"Don't know, but it sure is moving fast."

He'd no sooner spoken than the glow resolved itself into the shape of an animal. A dog. A small dog with an oddly shaped mouth.

Both men froze as the dog raced past them. They followed the dog's progress as it shot into the trees in the direction of the clubhouse.

"Did you see that?"

The older man nodded, not sure what to think.

'A dog?"

Again, the older man nodded.

"What was in its mouth?"

"It looked like a golf ball."

* * * * *

As the applause died down for the third place winners, McTavish stepped back to the podium.

"Our next recipients earned our second place honors through hard work and cagey play," the man proclaimed, "and would have surely taken first place were it not for a few poorly played shots, and the scoring legerdemain of this year's champions."

The room became deadly quiet, no one certain how to react to the wiry Scot openly impugning Muck and his team. By all appearances, McTavish didn't care, and that emboldened a number of people to applaud.

"Even so," McTavish continued, "the second place team would certainly take top honors for ingenuity and inventiveness..."

"Not this," whispered Pearsall.

His wife waved him to silence.

"They gave us the first, and last, taste of interspecies golf, an eventuality I was honored to have witnessed, and just as happy to see go the way of a lowlander's sense of fashion."

The crowd responded warmly.

"So I proudly introduce to you the originators of the Van Courtland Glen Golf Dog fiasco..."

"I had nothing to do with that," protested a slightly tipsy Verdu.

"...and this year's second place tournament winners."

Dempsey, Pearsall, Verdu, and Clawson rose from their seats, waved to the applauding audience, and made their way to the podium.

Out of the corner of his eye, Dempsey noticed Muck, in all his Victory Tux splendor, arms akimbo, refusing to participate in even the most elementary display of good sportsmanship. The man won the tournament, for god's sake. Why not let it go? Why not be magnanimous in victory?

Well, thought Dempsey, screw him. He'll get his one day. Hopefully, I'll be there to see it.

* * * * *

Arnie P. raced up the fairway towards the brightly lit clubhouse. The sound of applause from the building was of little interest to him. What was of interest was the sound of his master's voice, coming from inside the building.

The Jack Russell stopped on the tee box, a whimper rising in his throat. He needed to find his master.

Behind him, his pursuers were getting closer.

He hurried to the side of the building, circling around a large metal box, where a man with long hair was busily working, his hands deep inside the box.

Exhausted, he sat down, catching his breath.

Over the man's shoulder he could see a doorway leading into the building. Was it a way in?

Not sure what to do, he waited. And watched.

* * * * *

"Still have a few minutes to go."

The older man was becoming just as anxious as his young partner, and the whole situation had taken on a surreal patina. Between the bomb sitting off to the side and the dogs howling, howling that was getting closer by the minute, both men were on edge. They'd each worked hundreds of shows, most of them together, but this was the strangest either man could recall.

And it had seemed like such an ordinary day.

The younger man stood by the firing board, careful not to touch the precariously balanced mechanism. They'd decided to move the utility cart between the board and the Big Bang, for added protection, and hoped that it wouldn't be needed. If the rocket didn't make it out of the tube, they hoped that the blast wouldn't be big enough to throw the cart into them.

When dealing with the unknown, hope was all there was.

The howls were definitely closer.

"Man, this is weirding me out." The younger man looked around nervously.

"Not long now," the older man intoned, hoping he sounded calmer than he felt.

"We may not have a lot of time."

"What are you talking about?"

The young man, whose breathing hitched once or twice, and whose face drained of color, pointed down the second fairway.

The howling was deafening at this point, but what concerned the young man were the undulating, florescent forms racing towards them.

The other man picked up a flashlight and pointed the beam down the fairway. Pinpoints of eerie luminescence danced through the light.

"Eyes," the young man sputtered. "Hundreds of them."

Howls.

"Hold on, now."

They could hear the pads of paws hitting the hard ground now, and clearly distinguish the heavy, labored breathing of running animals.

"You hold on." The young man made a move for the cart. "I'm outta here."

And then the glowing dogs were on them.

The dogs cared little for the two men cowering in the dark. Their focus was in their leader, and their leader's focus was on Arnie P.

That didn't keep the men from panicking.

The younger of the two men tripped over his tools, taking a header into the side of the utility cart. Rushing to his aid, the older man stumbled over a knot of wires, causing the firing board to wobble on its tenuous base. He turned immediately to steady the board, and would have succeeded had a Golden Retriever, in full stride, not chosen that instant to go over, instead of around, the teetering control board. The airborne canine hit the turning man full in the chest, and both man and dog tumbled onto the board.

The board, knocked from the sawhorses, fell to the ground, jarring wires and making electrical contacts.

As he fell to the ground, landing next to his coworker, the older man clearly heard the distinctive 'pomph' of pyrotechnic ignition and launch.

"I see stars," said the young man, clawing his way slowly back to consciousness.

"You ain't seen nothing yet," his friend said, watching the faint spark trails of the rockets as they raced into the soon to be gloriously bright sky.

* * * * *

"And so," McTavish intoned, "for yet another year, the team of Muck, Baxter, Pfunke, and Howe win the Van Courtland Glen tournament trophy."

The four men stood and approached the podium. Polite applause followed them on their way.

As the last man took his place at the podium, the evening sky brightened, followed instantly by a muffled thump and the gentle rattle of the large picture windows.

Heads turned to take in the spectacle of the fireworks, surprised that they'd started early. The only one not surprised by the fireworks was Muck, confident that the display was set to coincide with his receipt of the award. It was nothing less than his due.

Not waiting for McTavish to hand him the trophy, Muck took the prize from the table, held it proudly over his head, and began his acceptance speech.

* * * * *

"Damn it!"

Wolfe hissed his frustration. He'd hoped to have executed his plan by now, to have sent golf balls, willy-nilly, into the kitchen, and be gone. Connecting a couple of wires was all that was need to achieve his goal, but the wiring was not playing along.

Someone in the past had thrown a quick fix at the thing, doing a little creative rewiring of their own. That had solved their problem, but created a hit-or-miss headache for Wolfe. Working only with the light from the kitchen made his trial-and-error wiring exercise just that much more difficult.

Thankfully, it was dark. At least that was working in his favor.

Without warning, the sky lit up like a sunny summer's afternoon, followed quickly by a loud 'whump.'

His nerves already wound tightly, the unexpected light and sound startled Wolfe into dropping his wrench.

Another explosion with light.

Fireworks?

He was dangerously exposed.

The wrench tumbled just out of reach under the ball machine. He could just feel it at the tips of his fingers.

Wolfe was already in an uncomfortable crouch, but needed to get even lower to reach the tool. He leaned his shoulder against the machine, pinching exposed wires between his shoulder and the metal side of the box.

When the next firework ignited, Wolfe noticed a small Jack Russell terrier sitting patiently about six feet from him. The dog watched him, sitting patiently, like he was waiting for a bus. In what was to Wolfe the strangest sight of all, the dog had a golf ball held firmly in his mouth.

"Hi, there, fella."

The dog whimpered softly and looked anxiously over his shoulder into the dark.

Wolfe leaned harder into the machine, shifting slightly, hoping to add just a fraction of an inch more to his reach.

Behind him, he heard someone come through the screen doors into the night.

The chef had been in the kitchen all day. He was exhausted. But his day was over. The food had been served and all that remained was the cleanup. As the chef, those mundane chores were left to the kitchen staff. It was the perfect time for a cigar.

As he stepped into the cool night air, fireworks burst to life in the sky. As he looked up, he noticed movement to his left. Turning, he saw a small dog with a golf ball in its mouth, and a man with a gray ponytail trying to hump the ball machine.

"Hey," the chef challenged, as another series of explosions lit the sky, "what the hell are you doing?"

Wolfe, taken by surprise, shifted to see who was calling. When he turned, two things happened.

The first thing that happened was that, in shifting his position, the wires between his body and the box made contact, completing the circuit, sending power to the motor. The machine immediately began thunking and churning. Knowing that the machine was unbolted and ready for action, and that he was in the direct line of fire, Wolfe fell away from the machine, just as a rapid burst of balls streamed from the chute.

The second thing that happened was that Wolfe saw a pack of dogs charging up the fairway directly toward him.

The Jack Russell scooted past him. Turning, the UFLACADAC leader noticed that the fusillade of golf balls from the machine had hit the chef, knocking him back through the screen doors, pulling the light doors from their hinges.

The Jack Russell bounded over the body of the fallen chef into the kitchen.

Another burst of golf balls shot from the ball machine directly into the kitchen. He heard shouts of pain and surprise from within.

The wonky ball machine began chugging, and Wolfe heard golf balls rattling and shifting within the machine. It was preparing to fire another volley.

He should run, he knew, but where? The other dogs would catch him easily in the open, and he couldn't stay where he was.

In a split second, Wolfe understood that his only hope was to follow the Jack Russell into the building.

* * * * *

The shouts and screams from the kitchen turned everyone's attention from Muck's speech towards the swinging doors of the kitchen.

Between the raised, panicked voices, the sounds of breaking glass, pots and pans falling, and what sounded like bullets hitting the wall, it seemed to those in the banquet hall like a major firefight had broken out in the adjoining room.

Fireworks continued to fill the sky, rattling the large windows and casting irregular light and shadows throughout the room.

Reluctantly, Muck stopped speaking. He turned to McTavish.

"Can't you do something about this interruption?"

The Scot considered Muck's request. He looked from Muck to the kitchen doors, then back to Muck.

"Perhaps if I went into the kitchen," McTavish offered, "to see what the problem is?"

Muck nodded.

At that moment, one of the kitchen staff ran screaming from the kitchen into the banquet hall, blood streaming from a cut on his scalp, followed by a barrage of golf balls.

"But then," McTavish continued, "I'm not going into the kitchen."

People and golf balls flowed into the room. Those closest to the kitchen doors were pushed aside by kitchen staff anxious to be out of the line of fire. One large busboy, his feet tangled with a coworker's, fell into the swinging doors, pulling one from its hinges.

Club members turned their tables on end, using the large tops as shields against the flying projectiles. Even those out of the direct line of fire were in danger of being hit by balls ricocheting around the room.

Dempsey's table went on its side, too, and all of those at the table huddled behind it for cover.

"What the hell is going on," Wentworth shouted, trying to be heard over the roar of the room and the din of the fireworks outside.

Golf balls hit the front of the overturned table, their loud report catching them all by surprise.

Pearsall, closest to the corner, peeked around the side of the table, half expecting to be hit in the head by a golf ball.

Pandemonium reigned at the Van Courtland Glen Fall's Eve Gala.

Dinner guests cowered behind overturned tables and chairs, able to avoid the worst of the assault. A few brave souls tried to escape, to make it to the nearest exit, but were either brought down by a volley of high velocity golf balls, or tripped up by balls rolling around on the floor.

Only Muck, who'd been abandoned by his team, stood his ground.

There was no sense that he might be in danger. To the contrary, Muck was furious that his acceptance speech had been interrupted. It never occurred to him that the very singular, bizarre nature of the events unfolding before him could be anything other than a carefully crafted plot to steal his glory. It was an extremely odd set of circumstances. Too odd, he believed, to be anything but intentional. Such things just can't happen without a great deal of planning. Muck was absolutely certain of it.

Standing red faced and barely under control at the front of the room, dressed in his white tuxedo with the green golf motif prints, Muck was utterly convinced that what he was watching was a very clever, intricately planned conspiracy. He would have his revenge.

"I'll find you," he shouted, unheard above the confusion in the room. "I'll make you pay for this insult."

Pearsall turned from his crouched vantage point and addressed his cowering tablemates.

"It's official," he stated, matter-of-factly. "Muck's insane."

Verdu ventured a peek.

Muck was now berating his teammates, who were huddled in a tight knot behind the podium.

"The best thing for him," Verdu commented, "is to take a golf ball in the head."

He had no way of knowing that Muck's wife, hiding behind a nearby table, was sharing that exact thought.

Pearsall dared another look through the rain of golf balls and falling bodies, and happened to see a small dog race from the kitchen.

"I don't believe it," he said, the excitement in his voice escalating a notch or two.

"What?" Clawson crawled along the floor to see what Pearsall was talking about.

"Are all the gala's like this," wondered Constance. "I think this is quite exciting."

Veronica laughed and sipped the drink she'd managed to salvage before the table was upended.

"What," Clawson asked. "What is it?"

"Look there." Pearsall pointed toward the kitchen doors.

The dog had taken cover behind an overturned chair in the direct line of fire. Golf balls smacked against the leather upholstery of the chair's seat, bouncing wildly away.

"It's Arnie P." Clawson turned to Dempsey. "Travis, it's Arnie P."

If the evening hadn't been strange enough already, the thought of his lost dog miraculously appearing was just too much to believe.

"Cut it out," he winced.

"No," Pearsall insisted. "Really."

The man stood, rising above the protection of the tabletop.

"Arnie," he shouted, waving. "Over here."

A battered Calloway ZX Blue ball ricocheted off the edge of a nearby table and caught Pearsall a glancing blow behind the right ear.

The large man spun and fell at his wife's feet.

"He's hit," Vincent shouted. "Mitch is hit."

"I'm fine," the wounded man protested.

"You sure, honey?" Nancy Pearsall, concern etching her flawless features, tenderly caressed her husband's cheek.

He nodded.

The barrage of balls seemed to be lessening, but no one dared look.

Dempsey suddenly became aware of a strong stench that seemed to appear from nowhere. He turned and found

Arnie P., ears cocked forward, eyes wide, and tail at full speed, standing next to him.

"Arnie," he cried, reaching out and embracing the dog. He immediately regretted his actions. "You stink."

The dog chuffed defensively, then dropped the golf ball in his master's lap.

A golf ball, wondered Dempsey, watching several fly overhead. The room is full of them, he thought, and then he examined the ball. His monogrammed initials, slightly chewed, were on the scuffed white surface of the ball.

He'd lost hundreds of golf balls over the course of his golfing career, but this was the only one that had ever been returned. And then he understood; Arnie P. had run off to get the ball that had been stolen.

He beamed at his pet.

"Hey there, little guy." Pearsall reached out to pet the Jack Russell. Arnie P. rushed over to lick the man's face.

"Careful, Mitch," warned Dempsey. "He smells pretty bad."

"It's like smelling salts," the other man stated, trying to keep the dog's mouth from his nose, but the dog, so excited by seeing his old friend, would not be denied.

The room was a cacophony of shouts, screams, thumps, and one, very persistent acceptance speech.

In spite of the mayhem around him, Muck continued. He had worked too hard, too long, to ensure his team's securing of the Cup to let mere pandemonium steal his thunder. Even the roar of the fireworks would not be allowed to distract him.

Nor did the chaos seem to particularly disturb McTavish. He'd somewhere found a tumbler of single malt scotch and was watching the festivities from the relative safety of the wall just outside of the kitchen doors. Since his official duties had ended with the presentation of the final trophy, the stocky Scot was more than content to observe the unfolding madness without feeling a need to intervene. Sipping his drink, he found it increasingly difficult to keep a smile from his face.

For others, there was certainly nothing to smile about.

"C'mon, T.J.," Baxter pleaded. Cowering behind the narrow podium with Howe and Pfunke, Baxter tugged insistently on the right leg of the Victory Tux. "Get down before you're knocked down."

Muck sneered at his teammates. How on earth had he ever aligned himself with such weaklings? More to the point, he wondered, how on earth was I able to win the tournament, seven years running, surrounded by such fear and incompetence? I carried them, he thought, reaching the only conclusion he could. In spite of their best efforts to see me fail, T.J. determined, I prevailed.

"This is our night," Muck stated. "My night! I won't let this..." he waved dismissively at the chaos in the room, "...interfere with the grandeur of this evening."

Howe, dodging an errant ball, sputtered angrily.

"In case you hadn't noticed," the non-descript man shouted, "this grand evening of yours has turned to shit."

Before Muck could respond, a tall, slender man with a ponytail, dressed in the coveralls of the grounds crew, sprinted into the room, nearly knocking Muck over as he passed, hotly pursued by a volley of range balls.

"Watch it, asshole." Muck shouted after the man.

Wolfe, without missing a step, flipped the bearish man the finger as he dove behind a distant table.

"I want his name," thundered Muck. "I want his name, and I want him fired!"

"Let's go, T.J." Pfunke, his toupee skewed at an odd angel, looked pleadingly at Muck. "You've got the trophy. Let's go."

"Not until I'm done."

"Done with what?" Pfunke took in the room. Utter madness. "No one cares."

"I care!"

Howe shook his head in disgust. "This is crazy," he hissed. "Enjoy the trophy, T.J. You deserve each other."

Howe made a dash for the nearest table, and he would have made it except for a golf ball that came out of the shadows and rolled under his lead foot. He twisted his ankle and fell shoulder first into some overturned chairs.

Pfunke was about to go to his friend's assistance when he became aware of the howling.

It was a new noise, just one of the symphony of confused sounds filling the room. But the noise grew from a low, sporadic background hum, to a loud, threatening roar that rolled from the kitchen only slightly ahead of the arrival of the golf dogs.

Muck viewed the arrival of the dogs at the party as just another indignity to be tolerated and, ultimately, avenged.

He was so deep within his own anger that he didn't recognize the first dog into the room.

Cali shot into the room, followed closely by the other dogs. The lights, the people, and the odd sounds disoriented the Doberman. The rest of the pack spread out as they entered the hall, though they were less confused than the Alpha Male. There were, after all, golf balls galore, and the pack had long ago understood the importance of the little white orbs to the pack's leader and the bipeds, even if they had no comprehension of the value of the balls otherwise.

Like a well-oiled machine, the pack began chasing the golf balls. As they moved through the room, the people became aware of their presence, and the owners became aware of their lost pets.

"Mac," cried one woman. Her focus was on a large, black and white Old English Sheepdog in dire need of a bath, trim, and a brushing. "McNamara Murphy! Come here, boy. C'mon."

The dog, hearing the familiar voice, sought out his owner.

"Capo," another shouted.

"Jed!"

"Augie?"

"Poppie."

"Boo?"

Names flew around the room as quickly as golf balls, and dirty, smelly dogs were reunited with their richly adorned masters.

As the golf balls lessened, the new noises in the room were the sounds of relieved owners embracing their long missing pets.

Dempsey stood, followed by the others. Donna turned and smiled at the sight of Arnie P. held lovingly, but firmly, in Pearsall's arms.

What had been a madhouse minutes earlier turned into an Addams family reunion.

"Puff Mommy." Andy Norton, not believing his good fortune, blurted out his Samoyed's name as the dirty, pregnant dog trotted into the room from the kitchen.

The Samoyed looked to her master's voice, then ambled over to stand beside her mate.

Cali became aware of Puff Mommy. The female nuzzled and licked the Doberman's ear.

"What is this shit?" Muck looked at his dog. "Where have you been?"

The man in the Victory Tux took two steps towards his dog, stopping only when the Samoyed stepped protectively in front of the Doberman.

People in the room slowly became aware of the scene unfolding at the front of the room, though no one understood clearly what was happening.

Puff Mommy growled threateningly at Muck, a clear warning in any species. The man with the trophy, however, had yet to receive the respect he felt himself due, and was not about to take shit from anyone. Not tonight, and certainly not from some mangy, smelly mutt.

"Watch yourself, bitch," hissed Muck. He took a bold step forward. The Samoyed snapped at the man, her ears pinned back.

"Muck!" Dempsey called out. "Ease up."

"Fuck you, loser."

"Get away from my dog," screamed Norton. "Don't you lay a hand on her."

Which was fine with Muck, since he'd intended to kick the dog senseless.

Another step.

The Samoyed growled again, but took a tentative step back.

"That's right, honey," Muck taunted. "You'd better back up."

As Muck neared the retreating Samoyed, the Doberman began growling and snapping, positioning himself between his mate and his master.

"You ungrateful cur," spat Muck, turning his attention and anger towards Cali.

But the dog held his ground.

And Muck stopped.

"Come here, Cali." Muck's voice, deep and commanding, filtered through the festival of noises filling the room.

The filthy dog was aware of his mate's soft mewing, and of the bursts of light and shadow that filled the room, and the soft, distant popping of fireworks. The sounds were vaguely familiar, more in kind than specificity, and vaguely threatening, tapping into painful memories of the belt across his back and haunches, and the popping sound the leather made as it stung his flanks.

Mostly, though, Cali was aware of his master's voice. The tone and timbre had been hardwired into his brain since he was a pup, and he could no more ignore the voice than he could stop himself from responding to it.

The dog, head lowered, inched slowly towards Muck, never taking his eyes off the man. As he moved forward he became aware of the golf balls printed on his master's clothing.

Muck stood motionless as his worthless, ungrateful mutt inched nearer. He unobtrusively tightened his grip on the Cup, preparing to hit the dog with it. Somewhere, in the last vestiges of logic that resided in his troubled mind, he knew that he had little to no control over those in the room. They might listen politely, or not at all, to his acceptance speech...they hadn't paid much attention up to this point...but they owed him nothing, and he had no control over that.

But he did hold dominion over his dog, and Cali would pay dearly for his betrayal. The dog, in fact, would soon bear the punishment for all the wrongs, real or imagined, suffered by Muck.

Cali sensed this, but was unable to stop himself from advancing.

Others throughout the room watched in silence as the scene unfolded, bystanders at a slow motion accident, helpless to change the course of time or history, and perversely enthralled by the potential carnage.

It was Dempsey who first realized that the fireworks had stopped. A mere instant of silence that seemed louder for its absence, but there was an ominous undertone that rang through the silence. He didn't know why, but he had a strong sense that something was coming.

"I think we should get down," he said, more a thought in need of expressing than a message to anyone in particular. He turned to look out the windows, the only person in the room not watching Muck and Cali.

Donna looked wonderingly at her husband.

"What?"

In the night sky a bright tail of sparks climbed from behind the trees towards the clubhouse. Dempsey couldn't have known about the untested pyrotechnic, nor that, in the confusion surrounding the pack of dogs chasing past the Landino Brothers' employees, the tube of the Big Bang had been jarred from a full, upright position into a thirty degree declination firing angle, the near perfect angle for lobbing the Big Bang at the roof of the clubhouse.

The comet's tail moved nearer.

"I think we should get down," Dempsey repeated, his voice rising.

Heads turned to Dempsey, then to where he was looking. Even Muck and Cali were momentarily distracted.

As all eyes watched, the fire trail ended. It simply stopped.

McTavish, drink in hand, turned without a word and stepped through the ruined kitchen doorway. He had no more idea of what was coming than anyone else, but there seemed to the man little benefit to waiting around to find out.

To his way of thinking, the night was already one for the record books.

"Oh-oh," Pearsall managed to say, before a bright flash filled the sky.

* * * * *

It was later learned that reports of the explosion came in to the police department as far away as the Marine base at Quantico, some twenty miles north of the club.

The huge picture windows rattled wildly before cracking and breaking. Luckily, the thickness of the glass kept them from exploding inward, sending deadly shards throughout the crowded room. The windows, after cracking, simply crumbled.

The huge explosion, however, froze nearly everyone in place. Cali, startled by the sound, remembered the sounds of his beatings, and the pain that seemed to define his life with Muck. And standing before him was the person responsible.

Lunging forward, Cali's powerful jaws snapped down angrily on the golf balls nearest him. Unfortunately for Muck, those happened to be balls printed on the front of the trousers of his Victory Tux.

Cali bit and snarled, digging his feet into the carpet and backing away with powerful backward jerks.

Muck, with his pet Doberman attached firmly, and painfully, to his groin, began screaming and beating the dog with the Van Courtland Glen Cup.

Those nearest to Muck and the dog moved forward to help, but were unsure of what to do.

Pain radiated through Muck's body. His knee's buckled and he fell to the floor, Cali never loosening his hold on his master's balls.

Through his pain, Muck continued raining blows with the trophy down on his dog.

Someone raced forward and tried to grab the dog's collar, to pull the dog away. As the man pulled, Muck screamed, and the good Samaritan was summarily thumped with the Cup.

It became clear that there was nothing anyone could do to help.

Thankfully, it didn't last long. Just as Muck passed out, he connected a solid blow to the dog's head.

Man and dog went unconscious together. If someone were to take that moment to step into the banquet hall, unaware of all that had preceded that moment, it would look, for all the world, as though Muck had decided to stretch out on the floor and take a nap, with his family dog sleeping there with him. Of course, that wouldn't explain the profusion of golf balls, the ruined tuxedo, the battered and bent trophy, or the ever-spreading pool of blood.

The sound of sirens echoed through the foothills.

THE AFTERMATH

"The dogs did all of this?"

Lt. Stone Parker was a respected member of the Fredericksburg Police Department. Tall, muscled, and immaculately manicured, the man commanded respect. And for those unimpressed with his size or appearance, there was always his record. Parker had risen to the position of lieutenant through hard work, intelligence, and a total disinterest, almost pathological hatred, of departmental politics. His superiors, including Chief Wentworth, who sat sheepishly on a chair by the podium at the front of the room, had nothing but respect and absolute trust in Parker's ability.

The young police lieutenant looked in wonder around the ruined room. Workers were busy sweeping up broken glass, collecting linens and unbroken table settings, and corralling golf balls.

"They had help," offered Dempsey. He and Pearsall were also in attendance at the front of the room, though why they'd been asked to stay when the room was cleared of members remained a mystery. The man who'd requested them remain, Malcolm Swan, the officious club president and director of events, sat next to them.

"Aye," McTavish agreed, suspiciously eyeing the man in handcuffs sitting next to him.

Wolfe stared straight ahead, eyes defiant.

179

Sitting with the men, still radiant in her gown and jewelry, was Julia Muck.

"The golf balls were an inventive touch," McTavish conceded, smiling, "not unlike an Oban cordwainer's double-stitch."

All heads turned towards the Scot.

McTavish cleared his throat. "An inventive touch," he reiterated, but left it at that.

Swan smiled. "The fireworks were an added bonus..."

"...that blew the windows out!"

Swan's smile faded as he nodded. His head turned toward the workers measuring the huge window openings. It would take a lot of plywood to close out the elements.

Parker looked at each person in turn. What a mess, he thought. An absolute mess! A marauding pack of dogs, a booby-trapped ball machine, a formal gathering with more liquor than a frat party, and a supercharged fireworks display that, miraculously, hadn't killed anyone.

He shook his head in wonder, a faint smile capering across his face.

"What's so funny, Parker?" Wentworth squirmed uncomfortably on his chair. He was unaccustomed to being treated like a suspect. However, given that one of the dogs that had appeared at the gala was his, and that he had, in fact, been party to the whole golf dog affair, his treatment wasn't unreasonable. The five glasses of wine at dinner, however, had put him on edge.

Parker's smile broadened. He considered each person in turn. "It seems to me that what we have here is a confluence of events, the likes of which I've never seen before, and am likely never to see again."

"And that makes you smile?"

Parker thought about that, then nodded.

"The odds of something like this happening are astronomical..."

"...your point being?" Pearsall asked politely.

"My point being that there is no conceivable way this could have been premeditated. No one could have planned tonight, and if they could, I would dearly love to meet that person."

"That's good to know," stated Dempsey.

"What I'm saying is that I am hard pressed to find any plot, premeditation, or malicious intent to pursue, from a felonious perspective."

"So we're done!" Swan began rising from his seat next to Mrs. Muck. Parker waved him back down.

"Not quite," Parker corrected. "I find no evidence of a grand conspiracy, but I have found criminal activity."

McTavish nodded. "This rascal here," he said, motioning towards Wolfe, "deserves a grand flogging."

"We don't do that anymore," Parker shared.

"Civilization's overrated," the Scot grumbled.

"But I want him charged," insisted Swan.

Parker nodded. "We can certainly do that," the police lieutenant confirmed. "We have Mr. Wolfe on misdemeanor trespass, vandalism, and reckless endangerment."

"That'll do fine, Parker." Wentworth slapped his hands down on his knees as he rose, signaling the end of the discussion.

"Not completely, Chief."

Wentworth reddened. "What did you say?"

Parker smiled warmly, but didn't back down.

"If we pursue Mr. Wolfe, we'll need to pursue charges against Van Courtland Glen Country Club."

Swan swallowed hard. "That's preposterous!"

"What are you talking about, Parker?" Wentworth took his seat and crossed his arms across his chest, a pose he'd used to intimidating effect with his subordinates for years.

Parker was not impressed.

"The club, and its members, are in violation of at least three leash laws, half a dozen animal control ordinances, not to mention zoning and wildlife considerations that could conceivably close the club down for months."

"Months?" Swan looked to Wentworth for help.

"That assumes that no outside parties file suit." Parker looked to Wolfe.

The activist snorted, smiled, and then nodded.

Parker nodded. This might not turn out so bad after all, he thought. When he'd first arrived on the scene he was certain that what looked to be a number of small infractions would turn into a major problem. It wasn't until he began putting the pieces of the puzzle together that he'd tumbled to the obvious solution.

No harm, no foul, he thought. With one exception, no one had been hurt. If no one sued or filed charges, none of this would matter.

"So, if no one is going to sue on behalf of the dogs," he summarized, "and if no one is going to press charges, then we can put this all behind us and we're done."

Wentworth nodded, looking to Swan for his agreement. The club president quickly nodded, the relief clear on his face. Even Wolfe seemed pleased with the outcome.

"Not quite."

The voice was soft, almost lost in the background noise of the cleanup activity.

Julia Muck looked to Parker. "I'm not satisfied with the outcome."

Parker considered the composed woman sitting before him. The police lieutenant prided himself on his professionalism, but his thoughts about the attractive woman, though brief, were anything but professional.

The paramedics had arrived before the police. They had stopped Muck's bleeding and gotten him into the ambulance and on his way to the hospital as quickly as possible.

The man was in critical condition, but he was going to live. He would live without his testicles, and his ability to walk unaided was in question, not to mention playing golf ever again, but he would live.

All things considered, Parker reasoned, the woman had every right to be angry.

The police lieutenant nodded at the woman.

"Please forgive me, Mrs...."

"...Julia," she quickly corrected.

"Well, Julia. I apologize. I wasn't trying to be insensitive about your husband..."

"...Screw him," she said, her voice remaining calm and level. "What's going to happen to my dog?"

"Dog?"

The woman nodded.

Parker hadn't thought much about the wounded Doberman. The paramedics had moved the dog to get to Muck. Seeing the dog's condition, and being unsure how to treat a dog, the techs had wrapped the Doberman in a blanket to keep him warm until the animal control folks arrived. When they'd arrived, Cali was bundled off to the county pound for treatment and disposition.

And the dog's disposition was bleak.

"Unfortunately, Mrs...."

The woman cocked an eyebrow.

"...Julia, your dog attacked your husband. The law's pretty clear on what has to be done."

"Which is?"

"He'll need to be put down."

"Killed?" Wolfe was suddenly angry. "Why kill the dog? Why not kill his master? He's the one responsible for the dog's disposition."

"Watch it," Wentworth cautioned.

"Have some respect for the man's wife," added Swan.

"And yet," Julia smiled, "the wife is in full agreement with Mister...," she looked to the pony tailed man for clarification.

"Wolfe."

"Thank you." Julia favored the man with a radiant smile. "T.J. is absolutely responsible for Cali's behavior. What happened tonight was unfortunate, but it was not the doing of my dog." She looked at Parker, then at the men sitting around her. "I know my husband. More to the point, *you* know my husband. He's a cruel, selfish, narrow minded man with a wide mean streak. I have no doubt he would have killed Cali tonight, whether or not Cali had attacked."

Those who knew T.J. Muck had their own stories to tell of the man, and knew that what Julia Muck was saying was true.

"That may be, Julia," the lieutenant said, smiling sympathetically, "but the law is unambiguous about what to do with a dog that attacks, regardless of who is attacked, why, or how deserving the victim might be."

"But we've resolved tonight's events," she observed, "by ignoring any number of laws. Why not this one?"

Parker looked uncomfortable, but was unmoved. "I'm sorry, Julia. It's out of my hands now."

Julia Muck nodded and smiled. She turned to Dempsey and Pearsall.

"Travis. Mitch. I'd like to retain your services."

The two attorneys looked at each other, puzzled looks marking their faces.

"Certainly, Julia," Dempsey finally answered. "What would you like us to do?"

"For starters," she said, "I need to make certain that nothing happens to Cali. He needs his day in court."

"Absolutely." Mitch laughed, nodding. "I saw that coming."

"Good." Julia Muck smiled again, but there was an edge to this one.

"You're not done yet, are you." Dempsey couldn't suppress a smile.

"No," Julia Muck confirmed. "I want to press charges against the Van Courtland Glen Country Club..."

"...Julia!" Swan's protest was swift and loud. "Why?"

Julia looked to her attorneys.

Dempsey nodded. "My client will file criminal charges against the club for knowingly flaunting laws and ordinances that prohibit unattended dogs on club property..."

"...Mr. Dempsey," interrupted McTavish, "the dogs were your idea."

"True, Mac, and I fully expect the club to countersue."

"You bet your ass we will!" Swan was growing angrier with each word, but he couldn't quite divorce himself from the years of training spent catering to the needs and wants of the club members.

"My client is also going to file a civil suit for negligence, reckless endangerment, and denial of marital companionship."

"Don't forget emotional pain and suffering," Pearsall added.

Julia nodded. "Yes. Pain and suffering. I like that."

Swan glared at the two lawyers. "If you two go through with this, I'll do everything in my power to have your memberships revoked."

The club president was fuming.

Dempsey leaned forward, explaining patiently.

"By the time we're done, Malcolm, Julia will own the club, and you'll be out of a job."

"Don't worry about your memberships, boys," she said, winking at the club president. "Once I own the place, your memberships are on me."

Swan groaned.

Parker smiled. "I'm impressed, Julia."

"You're kind of cute yourself," she answered.

"As Mrs. Muck asked earlier, given that we're winking at the law on so many other counts," Dempsey offered, "what's one more wink?"

McTavish started laughing.

"What's so funny?" Swan's face reddened.

"Normally, I don't like lawyers," the Scot declared, "but I'm enjoying this."

Julia smiled. "So am I."

"All of which is fine," Wentworth stated, "but can we reach an accord?"

"I have no problem if the dog lives," Swan said. "Hell, if it'll end this nightmare I'll pay for his treatment."

"A generous offer, Malcolm." Julia reached over and patted the man's leg affectionately. "Thank you."

The club president nodded, his mood mellowing.

"Unfortunately," Parker stated, "it has gone too far."

Everyone looked at the man.

"It's out of my hands," he stated. "Once your dog went to animal control, records were generated and the process began. There's no turning back."

The eight people clustered by the podium fell silent.

"I'm sorry, Julia," Parker added. "I wish there were something I could do."

"Surely, Chief," pleaded the distraught pet owner, "there's got to be something? Some string you can pull?"

Wentworth shook his head. "If it was your child, busted for cocaine possession, well, I could certainly help, but this..." His voice trailed off.

Wolfe mumbled something.

"What was that," queried McTavish. "Speak up."

"Maybe I can help," Wolfe stated, raising his voice to be heard. He cleared his throat. "But I'll need some assurances."

"Assurances?" Parker was skeptical.

"Not for me," the activist clarified. He turned towards Julia. "I know some people at the pound," he said. "They can get your dog out and make the records disappear."

"A doggy underground?" Pearsall looked at Dempsey, who just shrugged.

Parker chimed in. "That's illegal."

"Hold on, Parker," commanded Wentworth. "Let's hear him out."

"That's it," Wolfe said. "I'll need to make a call...the sooner the better...but I need to make certain that there'll be no questions asked, no investigations."

Wentworth turned to his lieutenant. "We can do that, can't we, Parker?"

"There is just one more problem, I'm afraid." Parker looked knowingly at the UFLACADAC activist.

Wolfe lowered his head. "Of course, you'd know."

"There's an outstanding warrant for Mr. Wolfe's arrest in Wisconsin."

"Where?" Dempsey looked to Wolfe.

"Eau Claire."

"Never heard of it."

"A small college town, if I recall correctly." Wolfe searched his memory for details. "I was on my way to Seattle. I'd been driving for two days straight. I pulled into Eau Claire for gas, fully intending to continue on."

"Ambitious!" Parker was impressed.

"Stupid," Wolfe responded. "I was exhausted. I shouldn't have been driving. Anyway, I asked for directions back to the interstate, followed them to the letter, or so I'd thought, and ended up right back at the gas station. That happened three times. I'd ask for directions and end up back where I'd started. It was like being caught in a very bad, very pointless episode of the Twilight Zone."

"And you were cited for that?"

Wolfe shook his head.

"I ended up staying in Eau Claire for about three months. I established a campus chapter of UFLACADAC. Then one night..."

"...that's fine, Mr. Wolfe." Julia interrupted the activist, turning to Dempsey. "I'm sure no one wants to hear that story."

"I do," Parker stated.

"I'm sure you do," Pearsall smiled, "but it's not in the best interest of our client."

"Your client," Wentworth reminded the lawyer, "is Mrs. Muck."

"And until she gets her dog back, this man is indispensable."

"This man is a criminal!" Parker was not fond of lawyers, not an unusual state for a policeman. Pearsall and Dempsey were doing nothing to change his opinion.

Dempsey laughed. "Lieutenant, if we move forward as discussed, we're all criminals, technically speaking."

Parker glared at Dempsey. Dempsey held the other man's stare.

"Even you, lieutenant."

The police lieutenant bristled at the accusation, but was particularly pissed because it was true.

"But you said yourself that what happened here, tonight, was a singular, spectacular event, nothing more."

Parker reluctantly nodded.

"So let me propose a solution. We've all agreed to let the events of this evening slide."

Heads nodded.

"So, the club will cover the cost of its own repairs?"

"Hardly seems fair, Travis," pouted Swan, "but, yes, we can do that."

"And you won't sue Mr. Wolfe or his organization for damages or press charges?"

Swan nodded, though it was clear he was none too pleased.

"Good." Dempsey turned to Wolfe. "And you won't press charges against the club, file any claims, and you'll pull the protesters?"

Wolfe nodded.

"So," Dempsey stated, putting on his best lawyerly voice, "legally speaking, none of this ever happened."

The others were silent, watching the attorney.

"Then let me suggest the following, which should address Julia's concerns. Wolfe will make his calls and make whatever arrangements are needed to secure the release of..."

"...Caligula..."

"...Caligula. Julia, you make whatever arrangements you need to make to pick Caligula up from the pound and get him to his vet."

The woman nodded, relief etching her face.

"Unfortunately, Mr. Wolfe will need to face his charges in Wisconsin. However, in consideration of his assistance to Caligula, Julia, would you agree to cover Mr. Wolfe's legal expenses?"

"It's the least I can do," she answered, "and I'm happy to do it."

"And we're happy to take the case."

"Wonderful."

Wolfe glowered. "Are you guys any good?"

Mitch laughed. "Have you been paying attention?"."

"There's a sweetheart deal," sniped Parker. "Somehow I knew you'd be able to turn this whole thing into cash in your pocket."

Dempsey smiled.

"Stone...can I call you Stone?"

The policeman shrugged.

"Stone, you're to be commended for your thoughtfulness and sensitivity this evening. Someone less intelligent would have hauled the lot of us in and let the legal machinery run its course. Someone more political would have simply deferred to Farley here."

Wentworth sniffed derisively.

"That would have ended badly."

"Now, hold on, Travis..."

"With all you've had to drink tonight, Farley, you would have decided the best thing to do, the easiest thing to do, would be to devise some grand cover-up."

"Isn't that what we've just done?" Swan was confused.

Dempsey shook his head. "Not at all. My guess is that Stone is going to write up exactly what happened, explaining exactly what it is we've all agreed to, and demonstrate clearly and concisely that all proper police procedures were followed. He'll report that there was no coercion involved, and how the decision to forego any criminal actions in this instance was in everyone's best interest, conserving the limited resources and time of a busy police force."

A faint smile crossed Parker's lips.

"And since Farley's going to sign off on the report, the whole thing will be open and above board, available to the public for review at any time."

"And what about the press," wondered Swan.

"They'll get around to looking into this, and there might even be some stories written about what happened." Dempsey shrugged. "The press has never needed much, by way of facts, to justify writing a story."

"You make it sound so easy."

"I'm a lawyer," smiled Dempsey. "And as to turning this into pocket cash..."

Parker reddened. "I was out of line."

Dempsey ignored the comment. "Mrs. Muck has plenty of money to spend in Mr. Wolfe's defense, and she won't spend much on it. And we probably won't take much, by way of fees, if we take anything."

"We won't?" Pearsall's surprise made McTavish laugh.

"We've got a junior partner from Wisconsin who loves pro bono work..."

"...McAlier," Pearsall said, rolling his eyes.

"...who'll jump on this and, in all likelihood, make the whole thing go away."

"I'd like that," Wolfe admitted.

"Thought you might," Dempsey answered.

Across the room, workers began nailing the first sheet of plywood into place. The pounding of the hammers thundered throughout the room.

Wentworth looked over his shoulder at the men wielding hammers. They would be at it for hours, he realized, and was certain that his head would explode if he were exposed to the noise for any length of time. He turned to Parker.

"Are we done now," he queried, "or do you have another surprise for us?"

Lieutenant Parker reviewed his notes. He shook his head.

"Nothing else, sir."

"Then I suggest we call it a night," Swan said. "Julia? Mr. Wolfe? If you'd like to use the phone in my office, I'd be more than happy to take you there right now."

Wolfe, Julia, and Pearsall followed the club president from the room, with Lieutenant Parker and a uniformed officer close on their heels.

"That comment about my drinking was out of line, Travis."

Dempsey smiled, helping Wentworth to his feet.

"I think it's important for your staff to see your feet of clay."

"I'm going to stick one of these clay feet right up your..."

"...okay, Farley," Dempsey laughed, leading the other man from the room. "I'm sorry. I'm sorry. How can I make it up to you?"

"Buy me a drink."

* * * * *

The club lounge was packed with well dressed, though disheveled, club members. The sounds of music...provided by the dance band that never had the chance to get started in the banquet hall...excited voices, and laughter were uncomfortably loud, though most were too drunk, and too engrossed in recounting the evening's events, to notice.

Dempsey, McTavish, and Wentworth entered the crowded room and immediately spotted Clawson and Verdu. They'd somehow managed to find and hold a table and half dozen chairs. The three late arrivals made their way through the crowd.

In the center of the table was an opened bottle of scotch and a half dozen empty glasses.

"We got a bottle," Verdu stated. "Not sure when you'd show up, who'd be along, or how easy it would be to get a drink."

Verdu and Clawson had half-filled glasses in front of them. Mac and Wentworth took glasses and poured themselves a drink. Dempsey took a glass, but passed on the scotch.

"To the gala," toasted Wentworth, sipping his drink.

"To the gala," the others echoed.

The five of them sat quietly, the thrum of music and voices washing over them.

"Where's Mitch?" Clawson looked around the room.

"He'll be along," Dempsey answered. A thought occurred to him. "Where are the women?"

"They went to your house to give Arnie P. a bath and have a nightcap." Verdu smiled at the thought. "I suspect there's more 'night capping' than dog grooming going on."

"Just as well," Clawson commented. "That poor pup won't have a shred of fur left if they scrub at him too long."

Verdu laughed. "I'll put my money on Arnie P. He survived the wilds of Spotsylvania County..."

"...the wilds?" Wentworth snorted.

"...and made it back in one piece."

"Smelling like a Georgia rendering plant in August," Dempsey added.

"Even so," continued Verdu, "aren't you glad he's home, smell or not?"

Travis Dempsey considered the question. What had started so innocently, with such naïve intent, had somewhere, somehow, turned decidedly wrong. The simplest of plans had turned dangerous, resulting in untold thousands in damages, and a number of serious injuries.

"Yeah," he conceded, "I'm glad the little guy is back. I missed him. I'm just sorry for all the problems I caused."

Around the table, heads nodded knowingly.

"I almost feel sorry for Muck," Verdu sighed.

The vision of the man being wheeled to the ambulance was still fresh in their minds.

"Christ," Clawson stated, squirming slightly in his chair.

"Still," Wentworth offered, "it does clear up one thing."

"Which is?"

"I always thought he was all talk. Turns out he had balls after all."

Verdu laughed, then immediately felt guilty about it. Clawson smiled, while the rest just stared in disbelief.

Pearsall appeared and took the empty seat. Helping himself to a glass and the bottle, he took a quick swallow.

"Did I miss anything?"

"We were just commenting on Muck's balls..."

"...or lack thereof..."

"And how Cali proved conclusively, and dramatically, that the bastard had a pair."

"Speaking of Cali, what's going to happen to him?"

Pearsall shook his head.

"Dead?"

Pearsall nodded. "Poor guy had serious skull damage. Never had a chance."

"Christ." Verdu sipped his drink.

"Probably the best thing for him," Pearsall shrugged, "given the damage done, but Julia's taking it hard."

"Loses her dog and gets a chewed up husband, all on the same night."

"She's more upset about the dog."

The men at the table nodded, understanding.

"To Cali," toasted Clawson.

The others raised their glasses.

Dempsey and Pearsall brought everyone up to speed on what had transpired with the police and the club leadership.

"So, after all is said and done, it's like none of this ever happened?" Clawson couldn't believe that there would be no repercussions for a decidedly unique summer.

Dempsey shrugged. "No one's going to jail, Muck may or may not walk again, and our dues will probably go up." Dempsey looked at each of his friends. "It seemed like such a good idea."

"Really?" Pearsall snorted. "You think so?"

"Well, maybe not," admitted Dempsey.

Those around the table nodded. All, that is, except for McTavish.

The Scot downed the remainder of his drink and poured himself another.

"Don't beat yourself up too badly, Mr. Dempsey." McTavish took another swallow of his drink. "You might think this has turned out badly, but you've actually done the club a great service."

Stunned looks greeted the Scot's pronouncement.

"You've had too much to drink, Mac." Wentworth reached for the other man's glass. The Starter of the Courses moved his glass from the Police Chief's reach.

"Where scotch is concerned, laddie, there's no such thing as too much!"

"So how do you figure tonight's not a bad thing?" Verdu asked the obvious question.

"What happened here was not disastrous nor deadly. Not too much so, anyway. And look around you. What's on everyone's lips, excluding liquor, of course? The Gala. Specifically, tonight's gala. What started as a novel idea about finding lost golf balls because you were too vain to wear glasses," McTavish said, uncritically, though his look at Dempsey brought red to the other man's cheeks, "has evolved into a major club event. An event that will long be remembered."

Clawson nodded slowly, awareness dawning.

McTavish smiled. He'd already secured the battered tournament cup, and knew just where to place it within the trophy case.

"What happened this summer, culminating in tonight's *ceilidh*, is one for the ages. Over time, what happened will be little more than a novelty to the current members, certainly those who were here tonight will come to treat it as a badge of honor...they were here the night the dogs, the golf dogs, came home to roost...but that will be it.

"But the story will continue, and evolve, and become so much more than what actually happened tonight. We will, none of us, ever know how the myth will finally take shape, and we shouldn't. Those of us here tonight are historians, bound by our presence to recite the facts as they occurred. But myth," McTavish said, winking, "is like a beautiful flower: A seed of fact, planted in the soil of imagination, fed with shite, and given enough time, blossoms into a rich, colorful, soul-pleasing flower that is nothing like the seed that gave it life."

"A rose is a rose," Verdu began, "but what that flower represents is so much more than its shape, or color, or scent."

McTavish nodded. "Exactly!"

"And you think that's what happened here?" Pearsall was unconvinced.

"I do," insisted the Scot. "You've heard of Stonehenge?"

Everyone nodded.

"So," McTavish asked, "what is it?"

Blank stares.

"Come on," he challenged. "What is it?"

"Nobody knows for sure," Dempsey protested, eliciting a wan smile from the smaller man.

"And that's my point," he chirped. "The Druids built it...they think...to worship the sun, or the gods of the harvest, or whomever...they surmise...and used it as a means of calculating the seasons...they imagine...but no one knows for certain."

"So?"

"So, what if a bunch of prehistoric pranksters, after a night of too much mead, decided to play a joke on their neighbors?"

"That's a lot of work," Wentworth countered, "for a practical joke."

The Scot shrugged. "Maybe they had too much spare time and were bored. What if they decided to get their chums together to put a bunch of rocks in the middle of Farmer Clive's field, just to get his blood up?"

"It took years, Mac." Pearsall was, by nature, a skeptic, and what the Scot was proposing was feeding his skepticism. "And they've documented that a lot of the stones came from Wales, and would have taken years to transport."

"I know all of that, Mr. Pearsall," countered McTavish, "but you're addressing the logistics, I'm addressing the intent, and the two are not in conflict."

Pearsall was stopped short.

"The point is that truth is shrouded in history and myth. No one knows for sure, no one that's alive, anyway. It could be exactly what we're told it is, or it could be a simple prank. By outlasting the laughter, it's become one of history's grandest mysteries."

"That's lyric, Mac." Pearsall was impressed

The small man nodded.

"So, you think we've created a Stonehenge?"

"Don't be daft," chided the Scot. "You've done nothing so grand. It was just an example." He considered his drink, the clear amber liquid catching the light through the cut facets of the glass. "What you've done is bring about a series of events that are notable for their uniqueness. You've laid the foundation for an epic story. Few are ever aware that they've contributed to, much less created, myth. You're to be commended."

"Here, here," Verdu cheered. He raised his glass.

"Wait a minute, Mac." Clawson massaged his temples. "If we can't know that we've created a myth, how can we be sure?"

"You can't ever be sure," McTavish laughed. "But I am."

"Well, that makes it all better," Pearsall stated, eyes bulging in disbelief.

"I still say he's had too much to drink," insisted Wentworth, sounding both very tired and very drunk.

"Think as you will," McTavish said. He downed the remains of his drink. Standing, he bowed slightly to the men at the table. "It's time for me to be on my way."

"Me, too," Wentworth stated. "Can I give you a ride?"

"You're too drunk to drive, Farley." Dempsey pointed out the obvious.

"I know that, Travis. I was going to have one of my boys drive me home." He turned towards the door at the far side of the room. "This is a crime scene, for god's sake. There should still be one or two police around, don't you think?"

"If you'll let me run the siren," McTavish stated, offering a steadying hand to the Police Chief, "I'll take that ride."

"Hell," Wentworth said, letting the small Scot lead him through the crowd, "you can fire the riot gun out the window for all I care."

The two men were swallowed by the crowd.

"What a bunch of crap," Pearsall declared.

"Golf dogs or Stonehenge?"

Pearsall thought about it, then relented.

"Screw it," he said. "Maybe what happened *will* become myth. We'll never know, so I'm not going to worry about it."

"Well said, my tall, inebriated friend." Verdu patted Pearsall on the back.

"Thanks."

Dempsey laughed. "The next time I come up with some hair brained idea, one of you guys stop me, okay?"

"We tried."

"Try harder."

"Absolutely," agreed Pearsall. "Of course, had we known about the dogs before you mentioned it to McTavish, all of this might have been avoided."

"Yeah," Clawson agreed. "Dogs were a terrible idea."

"I see that now," conceded Dempsey.

"We should have used birds."

"What?"

"Specifically, parrots." Clawson sipped his drink as he stared thoughtfully off into the distance.

"What are you talking about?" Pearsall and Verdu exchanged confused looks.

"Quit kidding, Rex."

"I'm not kidding," the Southerner insisted. "They're smart, easily trained, and aren't big enough to run off with your balls."

"How do you know so much about parrots," asked Dempsey.

"I own three of them," he stated. He leaned forward, conspiracy twinkling in his eyes. "And I know where we can get each of you a couple of your own."

"Parrots?"

"If we start training them now," the Southerner slurred, "they should be ready by spring."

"I don't believe this," Verdu chuckled, pouring another two fingers of scotch.

"No," Clawson insisted, his voice rising above the laughter of his friends, "this could work."

THE END

ABOUT THE AUTHOR

Buzz Rettig lives in Norther Virginia and currently works as a government consultant.

Made in the USA
Middletown, DE
24 August 2021